I0735551

A Jinn's Wish

Book 3 of
The Hidden Wishes Series

A GameLit Novel

By

Tao Wong

Copyright

This is a work of fiction. Names, characters, businesses, places, events and incidents are either the products of the author's imagination or used in a fictitious manner. Any resemblance to actual persons, living or dead, or actual events is purely coincidental.

This book is licensed for your personal enjoyment only. This book may not be re-sold or given away to other people. If you would like to share this book with another person, please purchase an additional copy for each recipient. If you're reading this book and did not purchase it, or it was not purchased for your use only, then please return to your favorite book retailer and purchase your own copy. Thank you for respecting the hard work of this author.

A Jinn's Wish
Copyright © 2019 Tao Wong. All rights reserved.
Copyright © 2019 Sarah Anderson Cover Designer

A Starlit Publishing Book
Published by Starlit Publishing
PO Box 30035
High Park PO
Toronto, ON
M6P 3K0
Canada

www.starlitpublishing.com

Ebook ISBN: 9781989458396
Paperback ISBN: 9781989458679

Books in the
Hidden Wishes series

A Gamer's Wish
A Squire's Wish
A Jinn's Wish

Contents

Chapter 1

Magic was wonderful, amazing, and awe-inspiring. It could destroy buildings, find lost keys, and raise a sunken ship with equal ease. Magic's only limits were the boundaries of life and the imagination and skill of its user. And even the first was arguable.

"So why is it I'm still doing dishes by hand?" I grumbled as I finished washing the bubbles from the last plate then dropped it onto the drying rack with a tinkle of glass. The small kitchen I was in held the remnants of our breakfast—store-bought frozen waffles and real maple syrup—the delectable smells lingering in the air. Cream walls and ten-year-old appliances surround me while I finish cleaning up and I wish once again there was enough money—and space—to put in a dishwasher.

"Careful. Don't chip them!" The black-haired, olive-skinned beauty I'd directed my question to didn't even look up from her video game. Some awe-inspiring, open box RPG world. More research according to Lily, but I knew it was more of an addiction. More of her way of adjusting to a world that had changed in the last fifty years of captivity in her ring.

Oh, yeah. Lily's a jinn, and until I'd released her four years ago, she'd been stuck in her ring in an abandoned briefcase. How one of the world's most powerful artifacts had found itself in an abandoned briefcase—untouched, unopened, and unknown for decades—was a mystery I had yet to solve. If someone knew—and I was sure someone did—they'd refused to tell me.

"I'd just Repair them. I got that spell down pat."

"Just because you can doesn't mean you should." Lily's tongue stuck out for a second as a stray lock of hair fell over an eye. She scrunched up her face as she focused on a platform hop between a swaying bridge and a cliff, releasing a breath of relief as she managed it. A quick flick of her finger put the game on hold. A glance showed her continuing to transition between hyper gates on her other computer. "You've grown to rely on magic too much. Magic's an infinitely adjustable tool, but sometimes, using your hands is better. Knowing when to stop relying on magic is just as important."

I sniffed, shaking my head. "What's the point of having magic if you aren't using it?"

"To brush your teeth?"

"I was working on my fine control!"

"Getting yourself a cup of water in the middle of the night?"

"It was…" My voice dropped as I winced slightly. "Cold. My bed was warm."

"And you used four different spells to get yourself that cup."

"Just three!" I protested. Scry to shift my point of view so I could see the cup from downstairs. Levitate to move the cup. And Light because I hadn't bothered to switch on the lights.

"You forgot your Force Fingers."

To turn on the tap, of course. I'd forgotten about that. A few years ago, splitting my focus to cast four spells, even four cantrip level spells like this, would have been impossible. I'd made great strides, but maybe I had gotten a little lazy. But... "It's not as if magic is addictive. Or doing harm to my body to wield."

Lily huffed and crossed her arms. "I told you before, it's a matter of mental flexibility. If all you can see is how to use magic, you stop seeing any solutions except for a magical fix. If you want to become the strongest, you can't be limited—even by your own thoughts."

My lips curled up, a sneer forming as I instinctively fought against her recommendation. That I had fought and lost this argument already was part of the reason why I felt rather petty about this entire thing. I understood her point, probably even agreed with it to some extent. But it was a conceptual idea, one that had no real bearing on me at the moment. The kind of research and spell creation she was speaking about was for the Archmages, individuals who, if I used my own little cheat System, would be in the high hundreds. As for me, I was a measly Level 63.

Seeing that she had won, Lily turned back to her game. Before I could decide on my next step, rapid knocks came on my door. As I threw open the door, I was surprised to see Shane, a deep frown creasing his short, bearded stature. It'd been

---

ages since I'd seen him—not since I'd managed to put a tracking enchantment on Charlie's collar, allowing Shane to track his cat. It was one of my better enchantments, especially since it drew its power source from the ambient Mana of the world.

"What's wrong?"

"There's... well. Better to show you."

"Charlie okay?" I said as I grabbed my coat off its hook.

Shane bobbed his head and stepped out. I followed the taciturn dwarf as he headed down the street. As we walked, I noticed how Shane kept turning his head, deep-set eyes growing deeper as he spotted our watchers.

"Don't worry about them," I said. "They're keeping an eye out for me."

"How many?"

"Five? No. Six groups now." I let out a huff of exasperation. Among them, the Mage Council, the Knights Templar, the Uttara Mīmāṃsā, and the FBI watched us from the various houses lining the street. I was somewhat amused that the majority of this street, and a portion of the neighborhood, had become supernatural central. "Forgot about the Druids. They're the latest."

"Druids?" Shane twitched, hunching lower. I wondered what the story was there.

I shook my head. "Don't worry about it. It's a long time before they'll do anything. In fact, this is probably the safest street in the city."

Shane grunted in acknowledgement.

I was no longer surprised by the details your generic supernatural denizen knew about my situation. One thing I'd learnt about the supernatural world was they gossiped worse than a group of mahjong players. Seriously, you'd think it was a superpower among the supernatural. But if you considered that even the biggest supernatural population was only the size of a small town, the gossip made sense. When there wasn't much in terms of laws and bureaucracy to fall upon, reputation and knowledge became the currency everyone banked on.

"Safer…" Shane fell silent.

I couldn't help but notice his body language, the way he hunched in a little, the way he kept sending glances towards me. Running around playing troubleshooter has meant that I've had to learn to read people a little better. It's surprising how much body language stays the same, even across supernatural barriers. But that might be a result of everyone forced to interact with one another constantly.

Eventually, we left my neighborhood and headed not for his, but another nearby street. There, the buildings were a mix of ground-floor retail and two-story apartment complexes, keeping the street vibrant and busy. At least, during the weekends. Weekdays, like today, things were a little quieter, though not quiet. Bisecting Spruce Street were numerous alleyways, and it was down one of those alleys Shane took me.

As we walked down the dumpster-filled alley, I couldn't help but look around. Sad to say, my life had changed significantly enough that wandering down strange alleys and looking for trouble wasn't that uncommon. From goblins living in the trash to devil rats, alleyways and garbage dumpsters were a thing.

My increased alertness was the reason I sensed the shift in Shane's demeanor. I was looking his way when he turned and plunged a knife into my chest, going straight for my heart. I shifted aside enough to avoid sudden death, but not enough to stop him from putting a bleeding hole into my lungs and tearing open a portion of my chest. A reflexive Mana Bolt punched Shane back, sending him stumbling into the wall. As if the attack was a sign, the dwarf rippled, his body elongating and lengthening even as his skin lost color and his beard shed.

"Doppelganger," I snarled.

My Force Shield caught his lunge, turning the blade. Not that the not-Shane gave me enough time to catch my breath before he stabbed at me while I clutched my wound. Only the training and the numerous near-death experiences I'd had allowed me to keep my focus on my spell. Well, that and the cheat spells Lily had stuck in my mind, allowing me to call them forth at a snap. Even so, it was all I could do to hold him off with one hand and keep my wound closed with the other.

"Time to die, warlock." The doppelganger kept attacking with one hand, but I was surprised to see him pull out an all-too-mundane grenade with the other. He stopped long enough to pull the pin on the grenade.

I was grateful for his mistake, as adjusting an existing shield was easier than casting a new one. The math, the change in the ritual runes in my mind expanded the Force Shield and curved it, making it a semi-solid, concave shield that faced the monster. Then I shrank it as fast as I could around the doppelganger even as he lobbed the grenade at me.

The too-large eyes of the grey humanoid widened in surprise and fear as the grenade bounced back. He turned to run, an action that I mimicked in order to back off as fast as I could. I did my best to contain and redirect the fury of the explosion, guiding the shrapnel and fire at my opponent, but my shield could only hold so long. And then I was on my back, staring at the stars, my ears ringing from the noise, bleeding out.

As I lay there, I couldn't help but wonder who had sent an assassin after me.

***

By the time my "guardians" arrived, I had managed to stop the bleeding with a Greater Heal spell. The accelerated healing spell started by clotting my wounds then slowly stitching the wounds closed as I held myself together. Of course, it left a big scar, but at this point, scarring was pretty much a given. Over the past few years, I had only managed to ensure that my face and neck were free of major scarring, allowing me to visit my family without serious questions. Well—except the one time I turned down a visit to the beach.

Greater Heal Cast
Synchronicity: 84%

A rather pitiful synchronicity rate, especially after so long, but I was still struggling with that spell. But unlike my normal heal spell, it had the advantage of fixing minor problems like a flooding lung.

"Wizard Tsien, do you require additional healing?" The Templar standing over me was giving me the stink-eye. He was in full tactical battle-gear, ranging from a Kevlar vest with multiple pockets, a couple of knives, a spiked stake with silver and wood, and of course, guns. Lots of guns. No sword, though the knife strapped to his thigh was big enough to be considered a short sword.

Ever since Alexa left the Templars, our brief interactions have been less than friendly.

"I'll live." I staggered to my feet, pressing at my wounds and looking at my bloody clothing.

Thankfully, I'd remembered to bring my damn bag containing an extra set of clothes. Over the years, I'd had every kind of body fluid splashed, vomited, and thrown onto me. An extra set of clothes, carefully wrapped and sealed in an extra-large ziplock bag, was a minimum requirement for my lifestyle. Though getting stabbed by a friend was a new one. "Is Shane…?"

"Dead." The reply came from the Druid walking over.

You'd think a Druid would be an old man with a long, white beard and a grey or green robe. Nope. The Druid set to guard me had a carefully manicured, villain-style goatee, long hair, and mascara. Add the leather jacket with the many little spikes on it and the black T-shirt underneath, and he'd fit right in a heavy metal concert.

"Not the doppelganger," I said, shaking my head and refusing to look at the mangled remains a short distance away. "The real Shane."

"Dead," the Druid insisted. "We put out a call for his spirit once your friend went boom. Got a return signal, all strong and angry."

I swore and, having felt my body settle down a little more, began another Greater Heal. My guardians ignored my casting, paying more attention to the corpse and muttering to one another. I would have been grumpy about that, but they didn't really care what state I was in when I reached Level 100 and freed myself from my wish to Lily. It would probably be even better if I was a completely broken wreck since they still needed to kill me. Which, you can guess, was why I was a little concerned that they may have let the doppelganger in on purpose.

"*Did you sense him?*" the Templar muttered to the Druid.

"*No. Our spirits were distracted. There was another attack.*" The Druid gestured around, shaking his head. "*We only had a minor spirit watching the target.*"

"*Heat signature was correct. Dwarves and doppelgangers run hot, which is probably why they chose him,*" the Templar said, running a hand through blond hair. "*No magical resonance because it was a doppelganger.*"

"Yes. We missed it too." Caleb Hahn, Magus of the Second Circle and my mostly reluctant Magic teacher strode over, followed by two hangdog mages. I assumed those were the ones set to watch over me. Caleb turned, saw that I was done with my healing, and fixed me with a flat gaze. "They tried to open a sealed gate in an abandoned shopping mall. Thus my lateness."

"I take it you've been having trouble?" My words were somewhat muffled since I was peeling off my shirt, showing off my no longer completely pale and skinny body to everyone. Due to the added training that Alexa had put me through, I was no longer the skinny gamer I'd been years ago. Call it a little bit of vanity, but I was proud of that. Of course, I'd be prouder if I didn't have a dozen alarming scars that needed hiding.

"No more than usual for this year," Caleb said, receiving glares from the other groups.

While the Druids and Templars might not like each other, they were both clear about their dislike of the Mage Council. It had a lot to do with the fact that of them all, Caleb had the best relationship with me—and the Council itself was warming to me. They'd begun to realize that a Level 100 Mage, fed spells and knowledge long considered lost, could be a boon to them.

Already, Caleb had advanced a circle just from working with me. Watching the way I worked spells, spells that had been lost to them, had improved Caleb's knowledge at a rate that left many of his peers behind. Even if he was forced to share his knowledge, because of his position, he was still leading the pack.

As I finished pulling my new shirt over my body, I caught a glimpse of the shredded corpse. As if the stench had been waiting, I caught a whiff of the body and gagged a little. If I could have backed off farther, I would have. "Are you intending to deal with the body?"

"No." The Templar was short and abrupt.

He looked at the body once more before he stomped off, soon followed by the Druid. After stuffing my sodden shirt into my bag and covering up the blood on my jeans, I glanced at the body. Better to get rid of the evidence. As I readied myself to cast an Acid Dissolution spell on the body, Caleb pushed down my hand.

"What?"

"The body will be dealt with by some of your shyer guardians," Caleb answered.

"Who? How?" I frowned. I knew I had other watchers, but only the three I'd seen already had taken steps to actually talk to me. Repeated questions had, thus far, offered little additional knowledge.

"I am not sure, though I expect that the FBI will win this argument," Caleb said.

"FBI?" I yelped, eyes widening. "Wait. X-Files?"

"I do not believe they have an actual designation," Caleb said with a shrug. "Nor am I sure if they are actual FBI agents."

"Then…?"

"It is clear they are from the government," Caleb clarified.

Seeing that I was standing, he walked out of the alleyway, forcing me to hurry after him, as did the lower Mages. From a quick feel of their auras, I assumed they were around the sixth or so Circle—not too close to graduating but not green-nose recruits. That they offered me jealous and unhappy looks wasn't unusual, but the looks were not particularly flattering on thirty-year-old men.

Repeated interactions with those in the lower ranks of the Mage Council had shown me that my name was mud. A lot of it was due to jealousy—not only did I get the personal tutelage of a Second Circle Magician, but I also had Lily inputting spells and knowledge that the Mages had taken decades to learn. I'd managed to achieve in a few years what they'd struggled with for decades, scraping and testing, experimenting. Add in the fact that I had a wider variety of instant-cast spells, and well…

Mud. Name.

"Clear? How is it clear?" I growled by the time I caught up.

Caleb didn't bother to answer my question. "Your Mana is low. You'll need to rest. We will cancel today's training. But you should be careful from now on."

"No. Really? I should be careful about doppelgangers sticking knives in my stomach?" I snorted.

Caleb just turned aside when we neared his apartment, leaving me to walk the rest of the way back alone. Alone, grumpy, and just a little worried.

Chapter 2

By the time I got back to my apartment, I'd calmed down enough to realize that I'd never asked a lot of the questions I should have. Among other things—who sent the doppelganger? While I knew that my reluctant guardians had been hard at work keeping me safe, I hadn't realized the level of enmity I had gained. However, someone sticking a knife in my chest was a rather pointed reminder that being ignorant might not be the safest option.

On top of that, there was someone else I really needed to have a word with.

By the time I opened my door, I was fuming a little. The front door slammed before I stomped up to the living room to see the placid gaze of my jinn—my real guardian, my friend.

"How come you didn't warn me?" I snapped.

"Warn you? Was I supposed to do that?" Lily said innocently.

"Lily." I point at my chest. "Stabbed!"

"I know," Lily said, her face sobering. She turned toward me, almond eyes fixing on my own mud-puddle-brown eyes, and offered me a sad smile. "I know. But I'm bound by the rules I set up as much as you are. I couldn't tell you, because he was an appropriate threat. He didn't have a gun. He didn't have a magical weapon. Just a knife."

"Which nearly went into my heart," I snapped.

Seeing Lily flinch made my anger cool, her words reminding me once again that the jinn was bound by the magic of the ring. She could twist and turn, prod and edge the rules a little, but in the end, she was still caught. I flopped onto the couch and traced the new scar through my shirt.

"I know. I'm sorry…" Lily drew a deep breath. "I wanted to. But I couldn't. Can't. You have to be careful, have to watch out for threats of your level."

Something in the way she said it, the way she wouldn't look at me, made me sit up. "Lily—"

"I can't say any more," Lily said. "But you're in the inn."

Silence filled the room, only broken by the hum of the taxed laptop fans. In the corner of my gaze, I noted her character being PKed, left unattended in a hostile zone. That Lily didn't notice was perhaps the biggest clue as to how disturbed she was.

I finally broke the tension by leaning forward and turning on the TV screen. "So. You know, *Ascend Online 3* dropped last week. I never did get around to playing it…"

Lily perked up, eyes glowing with enthusiasm. "Oooh! I wonder if they've fixed that long travel time bug yet. Everyone complained about it in the previous edition…"

***

That was how Alexa found us later in the day, when she made it down. Ever since she'd lost her income as an Initiate, Alexa had had to find interesting and novel jobs. Since the majority of her skill set involved killing supernaturals, her first year had been tumultuous. That changed when she received a job offer at Atlantis, the hottest nightclub in town. She worked the VVIP section there, keeping the various supernatural denizens in check.

Alexa barely gave us a glance before she performed her afternoon ritual of bacon and lettuce sandwiches, coffee, stretches, and more coffee. When she flopped into a nearby chair, she only shot the game a quick glance.

"Why is there a bag full of bloody clothing left to rot?" Alexa's tone was less worried guardian and more weary roommate. "We talked about how blood sets if it's not soaked."

"I think that shirt's a goner," I said. "What with the stab hole. I can't keep using shirts that you've sewed together and having people give me that look."

"What look?"

"The one that wonders why your shirt has a suspicious-looking sewed hole where your heart should be."

"Heart?" Alexa sat up, brows drawing together. "This… Spill. Now."

I sighed, hitting the pause button—to Lily's disapproval—and turned toward Alexa to explain my most recent near-death experience. The ex-Initiate was a good listener, only interrupting twice to clarify certain points.

"Both Lily and Caleb warned you to take extra care?" Alexa confirmed. She waited long enough for me to nod before she drained her cup of coffee and walked upstairs without another word.

"Alexa?" I called after her uncertainly.

"Leave it. She'll be back," Lily said. "Can we at least finish this quest?"

"I don't think so," I said as thumps and smacks drifted downstairs.

"Bah!" Lily sighed but saved the game before crossing her arms unhappily. A moment later, she let out a yelp of surprise when she spotted her still-open laptops. "When did I die!"

In short order, Alexa came back down with a series of folders. She dropped them on the coffee table before leaving to get even more. Curiosity made me browse the carefully labeled folders, only to shiver as I read them. The Illuminati, the Mage Council, the Knight Templars, the Druidic Order, and even the Council of Shadows and Dark Races were there. Every major power I could name had their own folder, some thicker than others.

"What is all this?" I said as I picked up the folder for the Mage Council.

Personnel files of familiar faces greeted me, each file offering a detailed chart and had at least one, if not more, pictures attached. Surprisingly, the files even listed their game data. Or perhaps, as I considered the information, it shouldn't be such a surprise. After all, Lily's game data was a good, if rough, estimate of threat level.

"Everyone and everything that has taken interest in you." Alexa said, tapping the files. "At least the ones I know of. Some are, well, a bit more circumspect." To underline that, she prodded a rather thick folder that just said "miscellaneous."

"You've been keeping track of all this?" I said, my eyes widening in disbelief. "But why?"

"I am your friend, you know. Also, I like to know who might want to blow up the house I'm living in," Alexa said. "Now, you said it was a doppelganger?" I nodded dumbly and Alexa frowned, staring at the pile. "Let's split them then."

"By?"

"Ability, then likelihood of using them."

I groaned but chose to not complain, taking my stack of the pile. In truth, it didn't take long for us to separate the various groups, with some—like the Mage Council—having the ability but not motivation while others—like the Templars— having no ability or motivation. In short order, we had a small pile of likely suspects.

"The Council for Pagan Religions," I said, running my finger over the folder. I noted the numerous smaller file folders contained within it. Among them, the Druids. "Tell me again about them?"

Lily looked at Alexa, who spoke while she headed over to the coffee pot. "A more recent invention. Until the sixties or so, the various pagan religions and magic groups worked individually. But the hippie movement brought a surge of interest. Rather than stand aside and potentially miss new recruits, especially considering how small the groups had grown, the Council formed. It has representatives from everything from the Druids to wiccans to Native American shamans."

"Wasn't there something about how the Mage Council and some of the other groups tried to suppress the Council members?" I said.

"Yeah. The beatings, Canada's residential schools for the First Nations, all of that was because the other powers were pulling strings." Alexa made a face. "Not that a lot of strings needed pulling…"

I grunted in understanding. While the amount of influence supernatural groups had on the governments of the world was not insignificant, most government policy was a matter of shared interest than a single power—or powers—calling the shot. In most cases, a supernatural group would work a bunch of human special interest groups to have policies come through. The problem with influencing entire nations was that you were dealing with hundreds, millions of people. And if you'd ever tried to organize a large dinner party, you'd know just getting people to agree on pizza or nachos can be difficult.

"So the Druids are their frontrunners for watching over me, but why do you have them in the 'potential' pile?" I said.

"I really wish you'd kept a sample of the doppelganger," Alexa said, shaking her head. "Without one, it's impossible to narrow down what it was you saw. Was it a fetch? A demonic construct using a physical change? A shui gui that took Shane's body?"

"Probably not the last," I said. "The shui gui inhabit the corpse. So it wouldn't have changed."

Alexa inclined her head in acknowledgement before continuing. "It could even be a Changeling."

"He was kind of ugly for a fae."

"Not all fae are pretty," Alexa said. "In fact, many aren't and just cover it up with glamour."

"So what you're saying is, because the Druids and the Council have access to these other supernaturals—either from their business or membership—they're on the list?" I said.

"Exactly." Alexa shrugged. "Low though. I'm more inclined to suspect the groups that haven't put someone to act as your guardian."

"Like your employers, the Dark Court."

Also known as the Council of Shadows and Dark Races. Among their many members were vampires, werewolves, naga, ogbanje, and aswang. The Council basically accepted any race or group that was inclined to "feed" on humanity and other supernaturals. Because of their liberal acceptance policy, they'd gained a rather bad reputation overall; even if they strove to police their own.

"Not the Council itself," Alexa said. "They voted already on the ring and weren't able to gain the majority they needed."

"Majority for what?"

"Anything," Alexa said, shaking her head with amusement. "A majority is required for any action. They voted to try to take the ring by force, to act as guardians, to watch you, to assassinate you, to bargain with you"—the blonde counted each thing off with her finger—"I think that's it. Anyway, there's a vote every month and nothing has come of it."

"So you're saying some of them might want to kill me," I said. "And they obviously would have the contacts."

Alexa nodded. "Which is why we should probably talk to them."

"Great." I shake my head. "Can we do it before the club opens?"

Alexa flashed me a sympathetic smile, knowing how much I hated those noisy, sweaty, alcohol-filled hellholes. Not that it had stopped me from trying them once or twice in a vain hope of getting laid. Of course, my expeditions had all ended in failure and an empty wallet. I'd admit that was probably as much a failure of my technique as anything else, but the added layer of danger from a supernatural hotspot did nothing for my desire to visit Atlantis again.

"Right. So we visit the Dark Court and ask questions. Who else do we have?" I said, turning my thoughts away from those depressing memories. And my rather long dry spell. Look, try living with two gorgeous women for two years while getting burnt, stabbed, and bitten regularly and you'll realize how morose a man can get.

"Well, because Lily gets banished if you die, we can ignore the majority of the dark cults," Alexa said, pointing at the second and rather large pile of individuals with the ability but not necessarily the motivation. After all, long-term planning wasn't their mainstay, and the desire to own the ring was their greatest motivation. "We're mostly looking at people who don't want Lily free. Or in the hands of Mage Council or one of the others."

Lily, glancing up from her computers, made a face, showing her distaste at the thought of falling into one of those group's hands again. I nodded.

"Which leaves us with… the Odd Fellows, the Alfar, the Kaaba, the Nine Unknown Men, the White Lotus and Blue Shirts…" Alexa read down the list.

I winced with each new name. Some I only knew from reputation—secret societies like the Nine Unknown Men—while others were powerful immortal groups. In a few cases, the names were individuals who had gained so much power—like Annanasi—that they warranted their own folder.

"You know, when you say it like that, it seems like more people want me dead than alive," I muttered.

"Oh, they all want you dead. Just when," Alexa said, frustration evident as we rehashed an old argument.

"Yeah, but not right now. This sounds like most people want me dead," I said.

"There's only one ring. And thus only one owner," Alexa said. "One winner. A lot of losers. And while most people who owned Lily were content to just use her for personal gain, now?" A shake of her head. "Now people understand how much she can do. And fear what she will be forced to do."

"I'm not that powerful. I mean, Lou and Mer would counteract major changes," Lily muttered.

"You're not helping your case by name-dropping them." Alexa drew a deep breath, probably pushing aside her irritation. "I've told you before, Henry, that ring is a weapon, one that no one is going to be happy is being used. The fact that you have a single wish left unnerves a lot of people."

"And also safeguards him," Lily interrupted.

"And protects you. But if they can remove the ring from play, they will." Alexa stabbed a finger at me. "Just because you want to ignore the problem doesn't mean it's going away."

"And what can worrying about it change?" I snap at the blonde, crossing my arms. "You think

I don't know people want me dead? That once I hit Level 100, when the wish is over, I'll be forced to fight a battle royale? But what can I do? I can't give Lily away. I'm not going to let her be traded around, used, or stored away because people are too scared. I can't train too hard, because that'll raise my level. I can't get new equipment, because they'll know what I'm getting. All I can do is wait."

"You could spend some time learning about your opponents." Alexa stabbed the documents. "You could pay attention."

I growled, shaking my head. Even if I did, how confident was she of the veracity of her information? And, even if I wasn't studying her books, I was certainly learning at my various assignments. But even as I did, did it matter? Many of these organizations were hundreds of members large. The people they sent weren't going to be the ones we knew. When they came, they'd have the information and tempo advantage. "It's not enough. It'll never be enough."

Alexa opened her mouth to protest, only to be interrupted by the beeping of a watch. We both looked at the watch Lily was shutting.

"And you're done. You've been at it for three minutes."

Alexa pursed her lips, staring at the watch before letting out a huff and ending the argument. I offered Lily a smile of gratitude, only to receive a worried look in return. Even if Lily, playing mediator had given us our time out, it was not an argument that was going away. It'd gotten so bad that we had ended up with this compromise tactic to vent. But… In the end, I found myself looking away from her too.

Maybe I was avoiding the topic because I didn't want to think about my death. But no matter how many times we argued, neither Alexa nor Lily had offered a better solution. If there was one that didn't involve magically wishing away our enemies, we hadn't come across it.

***

After everyone had calmed down, we returned to our conversation about those who might want me dead. The problem was, the list was extremely long and our actual facts were extremely short. Without the corpse and the results of any analysis, we could only work from the most basic of descriptions. And unfortunately, that description fit a wide variety of creatures.

A good two hours later, we'd gone through every document and website we could find and narrowed the list down to a half dozen types. None of which were supposed to have any real presence in the city. But globalization had brought about a large number of good and ills, including the globalization of supernatural assassins. No longer did you need to rely on the untalented and limited pool of killers and thugs in your locality. Now, with an appropriate posting or contacts, you too could hire an international assassin.

Yay.

"We're getting nowhere," I said, pushing aside my laptop. "Unless we can get the body, this is a fool's errand. And even if we did figure out who it was, it doesn't bring us any closer to who hired him."

"So what do you want to do?" Alexa said, slipping a bookmark into the book she was reading before closing it.

"We go talk to your bosses." At Alexa's grimace, I pushed on. "A good portion of our potentials are part of the Council. If someone came in, they should know. Or at least, be able to find out."

"I don't know…"

"I do," I said. "They aren't our only clue, but they are our best bet. Let's go."

Rather than wait for Alexa to respond, I strode up the stairs, grabbing my bag on the way. Upstairs, I threw in a new ziplocked bag of extra clothing, a traveling first aid kit, and looked around before deciding on grabbing my latest experiment. Puzzle ward blocks. See, wards needed two different things: the actual carved wards themselves and the power to charge them. The best option was to charge and carve the wards at the same time, to imbue the wards with the powers you needed. In fact, for the vast majority of mages, that was the only way they knew how to do it.

I wasn't the vast majority of mages.

Lily had dumped a ton of information into my brain, and after some initial teasing of the spell forms in my mind, I'd realized that many of those forms, especially when linked to a ward, were independently functional. That meant that I could, as I'd done, carve individual wards—the code of a spell—independent of purpose and power. They were just simple blocks, but if put together in the correct sequence, they created a new ward spell.

Which was why I had three twelve-by-twelve-grid mahogany wooden frames in hand with a series of carved wooden ward blocks already inserted for a force barrier and a ziplock bag of other "code blocks" ready to alter the spell. None of the blocks were as strong as a purpose-built ward of course, but it was infinitely more flexible. No longer did I have to carry around a single block for each specific spell. I could adjust the blocks as needed.

Though I also grabbed three of my one-use blocks, ones that threw up force walls, and added them to the side pockets of my bag. Sometimes disposable wards were good. On that note, I added an inscription pen, one that I could use on most materials to carve wards into barriers.

When I looked at the corner, I spotted my staff. The staff was a new project—a long, painstaking project—and my graduation examination from Caleb. Once I finished carving it, I was to pass it to Caleb and the rest of the Mage examination committee who, if they were satisfied, would graduate me into a full apprentice of the Council. Lily found the idea of a graduation amusing and insulting at the same time, noting that in many ways, I was well past any apprentice Mage. Though even the jinn would agree that I still lacked a bit in the theoretical side. My theoretical knowledge was patchy due to the way information was passed to me by Lily.

In either case, the staff wasn't complete. I'd added a bunch of Force and Elemental multipliers throughout the staff, making any spell of that form that I cast through it much more powerful. There was also space for a Mana battery, though I'd yet to find a Mana source I wanted to add to the staff. Or, well, a Mana battery that I could afford. On top of that, there was the usual array of Link and Scry spells to ensure that no one could steal the staff and get away with it. But major spells were still on hold—partly till I was confident enough to carve them in.

"Anyway, don't need the extra firepower," I muttered as I glanced at my hands. I could cast any spell I knew far faster than any appropriately Leveled Mage that I knew. Speed was my advantage, which was why the staff was geared toward offering power. And unless I was intent on blowing up a building, I didn't need the staff.

Once I'd mentally confirmed that I wasn't going to blow up a building, the only other thing to do was grab defensive equipment. I had two major methods of defense. First was my warded jacket. Of course, I'd been stabbed in the chest while wearing it, but that was as much because I hadn't zipped it up as any fault of the jacket. And second was…

"This still seems a little girly," I said, looking at the corded bracelet I'd beaded and woven before I slipped it on. Looking like a cross between a fifth-grader's friendship bracelet—with its bright colors and pretty beads—and a cheap tourist knickknack, the spelled and warded bracelet allowed me to conjure a temporary full-body ward. The hand-woven portion had allowed me to imbue my aura into the bracelet itself, while the individually engraved colored and metallic beards directed the force ward. It was the most powerful enchanted equipment I'd ever made, and it showed.

I just wished it wasn't that colorful.

Geared and dressed, I walked downstairs to find Alexa ready. The woman looked no different than she usually did in her work clothes. An exercise-shirt-cum-bra both lifted and compressed while keeping the chaffing from her thin Kevlar-and-chainmail combination to a minimum. A dark blue shirt, untucked to hide the gun she carried at the small of her back, and the enchanted bracers completed her ensemble on the top. Blousy pants hid space for knives in her boots and padded workout bottoms while also offering comfort—just like her flat, arched boots.

"Ready?" I said.

"Yeah," Alexa said as she lifted her gym bag. A gym bag that contained a variety of other pointy and bangy toys. Of course, a simple ward on the top of the bag made sure that even if we were pulled over, no law enforcement officer would ever pay attention to it.

"Let's go. See you, Lily." I waved goodbye to the jinn, who offered one too.

Chapter 3

In the end, we went to the only people who might know who'd hired someone to kill me. The Dark Court. Or the Council of Shadows and Dark Races, as it was officially known. With that kind of name, you'd think they would be dangerous. And some were. There was only so much you could say when you needed to drink blood or eat bodies to survive. Even if they played by the rules—taking donations, hanging out in goth clubs, or running mortuaries—members did slip up. And when they did, bad things happened. Mostly to other people until someone, like the Court's enforcers or the Templars, caught them.

Locally, the Court was one of our moderate-sized powers. Most of their members tended to live in big cities, finding the gaps which humanity fell through perfect for them. Large cities let them build subcultures and groups that rarely, if ever, interacted with the rest of society. Smaller cities made it harder, and villages… Well, let's just say there was a reason their numbers had declined significantly until the recent population boom. Even now, the number of vampires, ghouls, pengallan, and more were on the lower end.

Hopping out of Alexa's tiny blue car with its impressive trunk space, I craned my neck to stare at the back of the club. We'd parked in the open parking lot next to the club, behind the fenced-off area reserved for staff. An automatic glance picked out the half-dozen closed circuit cameras on the brick building, a slightly faded mural of a dark, oppressive woods at night facing me. It was an impressive work, more so when viewed through my Mana Sight. The mural itself helped hide the numerous enchantments painted on the wall, the runes of protection, detection, and reinforcement blending right into the swirling mass. It took me about ten minutes to note that there was no way I'd be able to pierce their defenses, not at my current level of understanding.

"Henry?" Alexa asked.

"Just checking out the building," I said, squinting and dismissing the vision.

The late afternoon sun beat down upon me, making me blink rapidly as my eyesight restored to normal. It was unseasonably hot for a late autumn day, which was annoying, especially since half of my protections were sewn and inscribed into my coat. Unfortunately, I'd run out of space for a cooling ward, meaning that wearing it in the heat was sweaty and uncomfortable.

It was no wonder that so many Mages dressed like professionals with suits and trench coats—the extra layers of social formality and professionalism were a perfect cover for the enchantments and protections we all wore. However, as much as I could understand that line of reasoning, I refused to give up my sense of style. If I'd wanted to look like a constipated professional, I would have become an accountant like my parents had insisted. No. I'd sweat in my stylish black leather jacket.

"Come on, you've been here before," Alexa said, grabbing my arm and dragging me forward. She stopped after a moment and frowned, tilting her head as she looked at me. "You have been here before, right?"

"To the most stylish, expensive, and loud club in the city?" I said, looking at Alexa as if she was crazy.

After a moment, Alexa let out a chuff of laughter. "Right. Sorry. Forgot I was talking to the introvert."

"Not that much. I have gone to clubs…" I paused as Alexa rapped on the employees' entrance, the heavy security door offering a muffled reply to her insistent knocking. "But this one's a bit out of my range. I don't think they'd let me in even the back door if this wasn't the day."

"It's not that bad," Alexa muttered as the door buzzed and she opened it.

Within, the club employees' entrance was filled with metal shelving holding everything from additional tablecloths, cardboard boxes of unknown contents, and cleaning supplies. The boring cream walls were a stark contrast to the glamorous main club floor, or at least, I thought so. It wasn't as if I had ever entered the club floor. As Alexa turned the corner and opened the door to the staircase leading to the basement, I noted that I wouldn't see it this time either. And if I felt a flash of disappointment, I pushed it aside. It was only a minor disappointment, one borne from having been kept out of places like this due to my class and lack of funds.

Down, down we went. We passed the mundane basement that contained all the wine, beer, stage equipment, and other goods required to keep a club of this size running. We did not stop, but to keep heading down, we had to be buzzed through the heavy security door and then again through another entrance at the bottom of the staircase. Behind the second security door was a small anteroom filled by a trio of cyclops.

For once, I was amused to note that the cyclops did not disappoint my old gamer geek instincts. Each of the cyclops was bald—mostly by choice, true, but bald nonetheless—singular of ocular persuasion, and muscled like a heavyweight bodybuilder. The only major disruption from my geek fantasy was the pair of shotguns pointed at me. At least the leader carried a club—an enchanted asp—but it did nothing to stop the sudden outbreak of cold sweat across my back.

"Alexa. The Warlock Tsien. You are expected. But I fear we must check you both," the lead cyclops said, walking forward while he held his hand down by his side.

"Sure, Nicos," Alexa said, stepping forward, only for me to pull her back.

"No. We'll see the Council without a search," I said, my voice flat. "We won't let you subject us to such an indignity."

"Henry, it's fine. That's the way we do things here," Alexa said, looking affronted at my sudden bout of stubbornness. "And Nicos won't do anything. It'll just take a minute."

"When you're working for them, that's fine. But we're here on my business," I said, eyes narrowing at Nicos, who had stopped and was no longer moving forward. "And as such, I expect us to be treated like the powers we are."

"Powers?" Nicos said, his single eye dripping with as much condescension as his voice.

"Ex-Templar Initiate Alexa Dumough and Mage Henry Tsien. Individuals with the strength to break all three of you without breaking a sweat," I said, stepping aside from Alexa and offering the trio a cold smile. "And while I can't guarantee I could take your Council, they can't touch us either. As they know."

Nicos's lips pursed in anger, but I heard a voice chirp in his ear. I saw the change in his demeanor as orders were passed over the guard's earpiece and the cyclops stepped back. A jerk of Nicos's head indicated we could pass even as the door out of the anteroom opened.

Behind the door was a new sight. The creature was dressed in a butler's traditional costume, but that did little to hide the lines of stitching that held its body together. Its skin was patchy, portions of different-colored skin stitched together to keep the creature in one piece, giving it a patchwork and pallid continence. As I stepped past the creature, my nose wrinkled as I caught the scent of formaldehyde and rot. The stench brought back memories of my grandfather's funeral, of his once strong, lively body laid out for the wake. The smell was only lacking incense smoke to complete the triumvirate.

"Welcome, Mage Tsien," the creature said, affecting a clean mid-Atlantic accent, spoiled only by the slightest lisp.

"Thank you," I said, stepping aside to let the sulking Alexa stomp in. I winced, knowing I'd have to deal with her later. Showing her up and putting her in an awkward position in her place of work would cost me. Probably about three ice cream sundaes. But for now, I had more important things to watch for. Like… "You're a Frankenstein, aren't you?"

"Yes," the creature said. "Bronislav at your service."

"Good to meet you, Bronislav," I said. "I'm surprised the Council has you. No offense meant. Just that, well."

"Most of my brothers and sisters have perished, yes," Bronislav said. "And few are created now. At least, not by the traditional methods."

"Oh?" I raised an eyebrow. "There are more… experiments?"

"Always," Bronislav said. "But the new ones, they are not Frankensteins, you know?"

"I think I do," I said as I recalled one pizza-filled late night when Lily had waxed eloquent on the different types of magical reincarnations. Alexa had her head canted to the side, listening a little to our discussion.

The Frankensteins were their very own kind, distinct from zombies, ghouls, vampires, and other magical undead. They were not empty husks given locomotion or spirits who were drawn back into rotting bodies to keep them in motion. Instead, the Frankensteins were a new form of life, given life itself in the throes of magic and science mixing, spontaneously formed through the doctor's alchemical mixture and the combination of lightning.

Newer methods of extending life via reincarnating the dead sought to bring back the dead. Unfortunately, more recent successes were but improvements upon the older forms of magic—spirits housed in less rotting bodies. Or in some cases, bodies jumpstarted and patched together to allow the spirits to survive. Revenants in bodies held together only by magic. But they were not new life.

What the doctor did was, as Lily waxed eloquent, a matter of chance and genius. Since then, spirits were drawn in, combinations of alchemical potions used, but to no avail. Life, like the Frankensteins's, refused to return. Refused to be born again. But knowing that it was possible, always did others seek to replicate the doctor's methods.

"This way." Bronislav walked us down the lounge.

Now that I was not looking at the Frankenstein, I could take in the room properly. The basement was more cigar lounge than hip-hop dance floor, with plush leather chairs, small coffee tables, and dark chrome everywhere. That there were few residents within was no surprise—like their namesakes, most of the members of the Dark Council were nocturnal by nature. In short order, we passed the bar and lounge and entered another hallway—this one more opulently done with red cushioned walls and dim lighting—to be led to a smaller room.

This room, unlike the previous ones, was a bare room, lit with fluorescent tubes and consisting of a single long conference table behind which the Council sat. That there were no chairs for us was a reminder that we were appellants. That a discreet but large drain was set in the middle of the floor very near where we stood was ominous. As were the dark discolorations around the drain itself. Rumors of self-run trials and punishments rose in my memory, and from Alexa's sudden wariness, in hers too.

"Never been here," Alexa said, her hand dropping to her side. I knew she carried her knives there, having abandoned her spear since we weren't here to fight. No matter how aggressive I might be.

"Doubt they bring good employees here," I said.

"I shall see you out when you're done." Bronislav bows to me and steps aside, leaving us to stare at the silhouettes seated behind the table. As the Frankenstein begins to walk away, he stops and adds, "And Mage Tsien?"

"Yes?"

"You are always welcome to visit the actual club. The bouncers will let you in. Though we do hope you'd dress appropriately," Bronislav said as he backed off, leaving us to deal with the Council.

Three figures sat behind the table—the Chairman and two others. The Chair I actually knew from having lit one of his family's weddings early on in my career. Eleventh wedding, and of that, a half dozen of those were to the same person. Vampires had altered the entire "death do us part" section of their vows, going instead for "till half a century has passed." After all, when you theoretically could live for eternity and were undead, a lifelong commitment became... challenging. And so marriages—or re-marriages— were a big thing among them. Having a Mage create the effect of daylight—without the burning and searing and death—was a mark of status.

Status, but not a lot of payment. Truth be told, I hadn't realized exactly how important it was back then and was taken for a ride, paid a pittance for what we did. But you lived and learned. In either case, the Chair was a known quantity, the oldest vampire in the city. Due to his age and wisdom—and yes, wealth—he ran the Council, but was known to be mostly diplomatic about matters.

The other two were unknown. One was a Native American, his skin the color of dark clay, eyes with a weight of blackest marble. Hair that fell just below his shoulders was held back by a simple stone hairband, and beside him, a cane sat. Beside the almost-normal-looking Native American was a full-blown green troll, a creature you could never see in normal daylight without a glamour. Green skin, at least nine feet tall, warts and big teeth were all present. As was a simple set of dark robes and a pair of glasses perched on its bulbous nose.

"Mage Tsien. Alexa," the Chair—Roland— said neutrally, greeting us as we approached and stood under the lights.

Now that we were in position, the trio lit up properly. If it wasn't for the fact that I could see the flow of power, the way Mana and light were manipulated to first put them in shadow, and now make us squint while revealing them fully, I'd be a little more impressed. Same with the way their words seemed to echo through the chamber. Tricks. But effective tricks, if you didn't see the enchanted wards and runes in the chamber. Nothing overt, just minor things to unsettle and unnerve.

"You come before the Council. What do you seek of us?"

I narrowed my eyes at the Chair's wording. Damn power plays. I knew this was going to happen the moment we walked in, which was why I refused to let them check me. Ever since it had become clear that the Mage Council had pretty much claimed me as one of their own, my interactions with others became complicated.

"Information." I paused, considering, but decided to play it out. "We seek information. And are willing to bargain for it."

"By the old edicts?" the troll asked as he leaned forward. That simple act was rather intimidating, when the creature leaning forward was that big.

"Hell, no!" I said, shaking my head. "One, I'm a modern-day kid. And two, I'm not an idiot."

"Pity," the Native American said.

I narrowed my eyes at him, watching the way Mana played over his body, was drawn in and escaped. The creature's aura was powerful, strong, but it was also harmonious with the Mana it drew in. And so, very much not human. There was too much "earth" in his aura, even for a shaman. Which, I was sure, the creature was too.

"Not from my viewpoint," I said. "A changeling attacked me. A skinwalker of some form. We couldn't get much from it before the Mages swooped in. But if anyone would know of a creature like that working in the city—"

"It would be us?" Roland sniffed. "Just because such creatures are under our purview does not mean we control them."

"No, but you've got your ear to the ground." I swept my gaze over the trio, trying to get a read if the news of my attack elicited any reaction. Unfortunately, none of them offered any obvious tells. Not that I would have trusted any such tells. "You can find out who hired it. I don't care about the creature as much as its employer."

"We can ask around. But what does the Mage offer?" Roland said, tapping a moleskin notebook in front of him with one manicured nail. Manicured or not, the slight unevenness and worn nature of his hands was a testament to Roland's background.

"Money. Or a service," I said, raising a finger. "By the new rules."

"We'll take the money," the troll said. "Medium-sized favor, current rate is..." He frowned, big eyebrows drawing close in puzzled thought.

"Ten thousand, three hundred, eighteen dollars on the exchange," the normal-looking one said.

My instincts thrummed every single time he opened his mouth, warning me that of the three, he was the most dangerous. I frowned, cudgelling my brain before finally I realized what the long-haired gentleman was. A Nun'Yunu'Wi. That was why he was so powerful. In fact...

"Medium…" I winced again. "You guys do payment plans?"

"No."

I sighed, reaching into my jacket and finding the envelope I'd kept my money in. A quick sorting of funds and exchange and I passed it over. Funny thing about working with supernaturals. Most didn't take checks, so keeping large stashes of cash—in this case, the majority of my savings—at home was common. Since so many of us lived in a grey market economy, a lot of money exchanged hands in that grey space too. I floated the envelope over, letting it drop onto the table with a thump.

"Thank you. You'll be informed when we know something," Roland said.

None of them even looked at the envelope. I knew they'd check it once I was gone, but trust and reputation meant that they wouldn't look. Not until later. But now, at least, we would have an answer. Maybe.

Because what I was paying for wasn't guaranteed. Just for them to ask. But it was better than nothing. I thought.

***

Outside, Alexa stayed silent until we were in the car and a block away from the club. Then she slowed the car down, pulled over, and glared at me. "Why didn't you tell me what you planned?"

"I… didn't think about it? I mean, I thought you knew that we'd be going in as, well, us. And not Alexa the employee."

"So it's my fault?" Alexa said dangerously.

I winced, knowing that tone. After living in the same house with the two women for so many years, I'd picked out a few things. One of which was compromise. Sometimes, it was better to say I was wrong than to fight to the end over something that might be arguable. And I did forget to mention it, or prepare Alexa for the problem. Even if she was, technically, the more experienced of the two of us. Sort of.

"Sorry," I said.

Alexa stayed silent for a second before offering a nod then flashing me a smile. "I am too. It's just going to be awkward now. And they'd only just started seeing me as one of them, you know?"

"I do," I said. While I and Lily might be loners by nature, Alexa was more of a people's person. She'd grown up with an organization, an entire orphanage full of people to rely on, to talk to. She had a family, a support system, and a faith she'd walked away from. Well, except the faith. That, I knew, she still held. It was just… different. "It'll be fine."

Alexa shook her head as she hit the button to open the car doors, only to pause as I was interrupted by a phone call. I frowned, a small curl of dread flashing through my stomach when I saw the name on the caller display.

Chapter 4

"Wei?" I said into the phone, offering a traditional greeting and inquiry at the same time.

"Oy! You. Call Mom. You've not called in a month, you know!" My sister's shrill voice came over the phone. Elder sisters were the same the world over, I thought. Bossy and always right.

"Has it been a month already?" I winced. I wished I could say I'd been dodging calls, but the way of Chinese parents the world over was they expected me to call them, not the other way around. It was my duty—which, as usual, I failed at. I really was not a good son. "Sorry. I'll do it tomorrow."

"You… you… you know what. We're doing dinner. Now."

"What?"

"Dinner. At the usual place." As if to entice me to come after berating me, she added, "I'm buying."

"Fine, fine," I said, wincing.

It had been months since I'd seen her. Not since the last family gathering I'd managed to make. Sometimes it was strange that I could live so close to my family and yet never really see them. I liked my family. You know, in the abstract.

In the flesh, my family was grumpy, insistent, and prone to a lot of guilt-tripping. Even if I did deserve it most of the time, I didn't want to be subjected to that kind of environment. Of course, there were advantages to showing up at family dinners—including my mother's cooking.

Once I'd explained the matter to Alexa, she insisted on dropping me off at our designated meeting place—the only decent Hong Kong dessert shop in the city. There were others around, but this was the only one that did desserts right. Whether it was because the store was owned by a family or because we had grown up eating similar desserts, my sister and I agreed there just wasn't another place that compared. Proper, pressed soybean drinks, hot tofu pudding with just the right amount of cane sugar, crispy pancakes with drizzled condensed milk. My mouth watered at the thought. Once again, I wondered why it had taken me so long to come back.

As I stepped out of the car, stretching from the long ride over, I held the door open to speak with my friend. "You sure you won't come?"

"It's a family meeting," Alexa said, shaking her head. "And your sis can get you home just as well as I can. Make sure to bring some snacks back for us."

"As if Lily would let me forget." I snorted.

Alexa chuckled as we regarded the Quest that had appeared in our joint eyesight.

Quest Received: Bribe the GM
Bring back delectable snacks for the GM.
Rewards: Variable, depending on satisfactory levels of bribes

Of course, we both knew that this particular quest wouldn't provide much in terms of experience. But bribing the GM was a long-time tradition in tabletop games, so it was "allowed," according to Lily. I still thought she was stretching the wish a little, but since it was in my favor, I wouldn't complain. Closing the door on the car, I waved Alexa off before turning around.

The dessert café was bracketed by large storefront windows that showed the fluorescent-lit interior. Within, multiple square tables lined the cream-colored wall before a single counter blocked off the dessert display and the kitchen behind. A pair of waitresses in casual clothing worked the counter and the floor. Students on a late-night food run, tired professionals, and a single four-person family filled the small café, but my sister was not among those present.

Having scoped out the location, I walked in and was quickly shown to my seat. The red upholstered chair squeaked slightly as I placed my jean-clad derriere on it and flipped open the presented menu. An order of non-caffeinated bubble tea later, I was resting quietly against the hard chair-back when my sister breezed in.

Terror of my past, annoyance of the present, my future berater stalked towards me. She barely crossed the five-foot line by a pair of inches, though you wouldn't know it as her three-inch heels took her from vertically tiny to just short. Petite or not, my sister had enough attitude to take up a room and the delicate features that had men clustering around her whenever she went clubbing.

"Hey, sis," I said, waving from my seat.

Katie—Katherine, but she hated the full name—took a seat and glanced at the menu. "You ordered yet?"

I shook my head.

"Good. You always get it wrong." Waving, she got the attention of a waitress and fired off a series of orders before turning her piercing attention on me. "You're looking good. Added a bit of muscle. And that jacket's new."

I glanced at the enchanted coat and shrugged, grateful that the enchantments were on the inside. Not that they looked like anything but weird runic glyphs, badly sewn or burnt on. One thing they didn't discuss in all the books and fantasies was how hard it was to actually do the work. I swore if I was in a proper game system, I'd have sewing at level 5 already.

"Thanks?" I said hesitantly.

"So this new job of yours is going well?" Katie said, eyes narrowing.

"It's piecemeal, but there's enough money in it." I knew the question was about more than money, though money was a big part of the conversation. After all, it was hard to be healthy and happy when you were struggling to make ends meet. Not impossible. Just hard.

"And what is it that you do again?"

I suppressed the smile that tried to creep onto my face. I'd been purposely vague with my family. Hard to say "I run quests, make minor magical items, and occasionally kill monsters" with a straight face. Among other things, my liberal, civilized, and worrywart parents would freak out about the idea of me getting injured. Even if I did have magically gifted healing, it was just a sped-up system. Not a hand-wavey fix.

"Arts and crafts," I said. "I make things and sell them to people." That answer wasn't much better, not for an Asian family, but we make do. "And run errands for some of my richer clients."

"You know what Mama and Papa would say, right?" Katie said, eyes narrowing.

"Why do you think I stay away?"

"Avoiding the argument won't change their views," Katie said. "In fact, it makes you look like a child trying to hide a smoke."

"But talking to them won't change their minds. You know them. Have you ever won an argument?" I countered, shaking my head. "Easier to just keep them in the dark."

"And at arm's length?" Katie opened her mouth to berate me further but was interrupted as the food arrived. When the waitress left, I picked up a sesame ball and dropped it on her plate. "This isn't over!"

"Food first." I popped one of the balls into my mouth.

Katie sighed but dropped the conversation, allowing us to focus on the dishes. In short order, we were done, replete and less angry.

"Henry, you need to call and visit more. Staying away hurts them. You know that. I know you know that, so why?"

I grimaced but stayed silent, not having a particularly good answer.

Katie sighed, shaking her head, and pointed at me. "Ever since you started this new job, it's been like that. And don't think we haven't noticed the new scars and the muscles. Are you part of a triad? A gang?"

"Of course not!"

Katie smiled slightly at how fast I replied, taking it for the truth it was. I was just grateful that I hadn't tried to overthink the question, since the Mage Council could be considered a weird cult. Not a triad or gang, but, you know.

"Then where are you getting all this money? I don't believe you're earning that much just 'running errands.'"

"Well, I don't care if you don't believe it. It's the truth." I paused, then added, "Okay, not just running errands. I get a bunch from selling my stuff."

"Your… stuff." Katie waggled her eyebrows, and I snorted.

"Not that kind."

"True. You have no chance at earning a living that way," Katie said.

I sniffed, but I had to admit I was grateful that we had shifted our talk in a new direction. For a time, we turned to happier things, like discussions about Katie's lack of a love life as she pursued her career in the banking industry, about old friends and past experiences. We talked like family did, about nothing important and everything. And I couldn't help but forget some of my worries, forget about the fact that someone had tried to kill me earlier that day. I reveled in the normalcy of the conversation, and my sister, the smart woman that she was, noticed it.

Eventually, the waitress gave us a look, hinting that it was time to free up her table. I paid for the bill, making sure to leave a generous tip. An act that made Katie raise an eyebrow, though she didn't pursue it.

Our congenial atmosphere lasted until she dropped me off at home. Then she put a hand on my arm, growing serious. "Henry. Call them. And… consider trusting us. Whatever is going on, you know we'll support you."

I flashed her a quick, wry smile and nodded, detaching my arm from hers as I opened the door. Family, obligation, responsibilities. I was never good at them. Not at home, not in person. But I'd try to call them more often, even if I had to lie. Because for all that I wanted it otherwise, might want it otherwise, my life was not one I'd drag them into.

Chapter 5

The next morning, we pulled up at the scene of the crime. Not mine, since that one was still blocked off by government representatives and my guardians. No, the original crime. Shane's murder. Of course, I didn't know exactly where he had been killed, but his home was our best bet.

We approached the apartment, having parked Alexa's car a distance away. The ex-Initiate had her gym bag slung over the shoulder of her inscrolled winter jacket. It was rather nice of her friends from the Templars to send that to her for Christmas last winter, even if the note guilting her for leaving had been rather passive-aggressive. Still, the coat was both armored and imbued with faith magic, such that she was better protected against malicious magic than even I was.

The flat was in one of those concrete block, low-income buildings that had been built in the 1960s and never really updated. Even the wallpaper in the corridors was faded and stained from years of use, no matter the amount of care taken for it. For all its wear, it was obvious the inhabitants of the building took good care of it. The floors were swept and mopped, the scent of a cleaning fluid assaulting my nose as I walked down the well-lit corridor.

Shane's apartment was one of the larger ones, a legacy of how long the dwarf had lived there. Staring at the green door, it took me only a moment to locate the spell ward that subtly turned away unwanted visitors. This one was still intact, traces of its user still glowing.

"Are we going in?" Alexa asked impatiently. Breaking and entering had a tendency to put the ex-Initiate on edge, especially since she'd lost the protection of her order.

"One second," I said, touching the ward. I manipulated it, pulling forth the ward's aura.

I nodded after a second, releasing the ward, having memorized the traces of the magical signature still left on it. The ward had degraded such that I wouldn't be able to track its caster, but if they used magic near me, it'd probably be possible to figure out who they were. Most likely, the ward maker was dead, killed by my hand yesterday. But… you never know.

After that, breaking in required two spells— one to bypass the ward, the second to open the locks. Magic made crime way too easy. It was one of the reasons why we policed each other so much—when the governments got involved, they had a tendency to overreact. Or, perhaps, because we never gave them a chance to properly react, they didn't have a middle ground.

When I move to step in, Alexa pushes me aside, shooting me a glare that I duck my head to avoid. She enters, the buckler she carried in her gym bag on her hand while a shorter stick was held in the other. That stick, I knew, could extend to form a point of Mana-imbued force. It was one of my better inventions, though the charge could only hold for about ten minutes.

It was a good thing too that Alexa went ahead, as three steps into the apartment, she was attacked by a crazed ball of fur. She caught the attacker on her shield, holding its claws away from her face. A few struggles and three deep scratches later, I had the cat suspended in mid-air, snarling at us.

"Forgot about Charlie," I said.

"I didn't," Alexa said, glaring at the deep scratches on her wrist.

She waved for me to deal with the feline while she scouted out the rest of the apartment. By the time she had come back, I'd set up a small force wall to keep the cat contained. Alexa caught me browsing through cupboards, looking for the remainder of Shane's cat food, when she got back.

"Do you mind opening the window?" I said, gesturing outward.

Agitated and abandoned, forced to stay at home—which he hated—Charlie had proceeded to make his distaste known. Cat urine, vomit, and feces made the interior of the apartment rather horrendous for all right-thinking, breathing creatures.

Alexa quickly complied then poked her head out the window, eyeing the fire escape before walking back, carefully. Shane's residence was, beyond its feline-induced chaos, relatively neat. The dwarf had been a collector of puzzle blocks and rocks. All across the room were mason jars filled with rocks, all of them placed in a haphazard manner with no sense—at least to my eyes—for the kind of geology they contained. As for Shane's furniture, most of it was worn and marked, the few cushions split, stuffing falling out. But beyond that, there was a mild discomfort in being in the room, one that I only twigged on later.

Everything was a little bit smaller than it should be. I wasn't that tall, but Shane was—had been—a dwarf. So… yeah. Chairs were a little lower, tables fitting perfectly for someone four and a half feet tall. Even the stepstool kind of made sense.

"So now what?" Alexa said, eyeing the content cat after I'd refilled its bowls.

"Now we look for a clue."

"And what would that look like?"

"If I knew, I'd have a clue."

Alexa groaned but proceeded to help. After we finished up going through the living room and pantry together, she relegated me to the bedroom, saying how weird it would be to go there herself. While I was browsing through sock drawers and finding contents that were all too typical, I heard a shout from Alexa.

"What is it?" I said, walking over, relieved to have left the bedroom.

"Appointment book!" Alexa said, waving at the desk she sat behind. "I think I've narrowed down his death day."

I nodded, taking the book from her. We were already certain that Shane hadn't died here. Death had a tendency to release a large amount of energy and emotions, ensuring that any practitioner of the magic arts could pick out a recent death. Unless steps were taken to disperse both the lingering death aura and the magic release. But those actions also often left their mark.

The appointment book was neatly organized, and it was clear why Alexa was certain of the day of death. Shane had a tendency to leave notes on appointments and on the day itself at the bottom of each finished day, making the appointment book part calendar and part diary. On the day in question, there were no additional notes—and it was also two days ago. Which made it well within our expectations.

"The White Scarves?" I frowned, tapping the only appointment of consequence. Unless he was taken while running groceries, that was our best bet.

"It's the Chinese group. Tong? Triad?" Alexa scratched her head. "Secret society turned supernatural group turned sort-of gangsters?"

"I know who they are. I just don't know where they are." I paused, considering. "One second." A brief phone search later, I nodded, tossing the appointment book back onto the table. "Got it."

"You ran a search on them? What did you type in? 'Supernatural secret societies, Chinese'?" Alexa said.

"Sort of, yeah. The associations are sort of like the Yakuza. They've got meeting places that are official and meant for their members to join. Clan associations, secret societies, whatever. Since the White Scarves aren't actually a triad, it was easy finding them," I said. "We should probably finish up here, but that seems like our best option."

Alexa nodded, turning back to looking around the office for further clues. As for myself, I went back to poking around the bedroom, checking under the bed, looking for other tell-tale problems. Only when I was done, finding little else but dust bunnies and a small safe that contained a gun, did I remember something important.

"Lily, don't I get a Quest or something?" I said to the empty air, knowing that the jinn was watching over me.

Of course, she couldn't talk to me directly, but I got a reply anyway.

Quest: Do What You Were Going to Do Anyway

Find the people who put a death warrant out on your head and deal with them.

Failure: Death

Reward: You live. Also, a Level Up.

The quest notification was within expectation. The reward was much less so. I felt my mouth dry before I swiped the quest away. Like any good game, rewards were offered based off difficulty level. If Lily was willing to give me a full level, especially considering how hard the levels were getting these days, she was expecting survival to be a chore.

"Why do I have a quest telling me to keep you alive?" Alexa said, catching me staring into mid-air as I pondered this new information.

"Sorry. Lily. Do we…" I licked my lips, and paused. "Are you sure you want to do this?"

"Do what?"

"Stick with me. You don't have to…" I trailed off as Alexa glared at me. "You're free, you know."

"And run off when my friend needs me? The devil take that." Alexa snorted. "Even if the Templars don't think I'm suitable anymore, the Oracle meant for me to be here. And here I'll be."

I blinked, recalling what Alexa said. And realizing that for all the time we'd been together, she hadn't brought up that. That reason why she had first come into my life. And yet, even if she wasn't an Initiate, even if she was no longer a Templar-to-be, her faith in both the Oracle and what she was meant to do was unshaken.

"Thank you," I said, offering her a half-smile. I hoped that she was choosing right.

We stayed silent until I got out of the bedroom and spotted Charlie, curled up in the corner and looking content. The cat had gorged himself on the food and water and now slept peacefully.

"What do we do about Charlie?"

Alexa frowned. "Did Shane have friends? Someone who could take care of him? Family?"

I shook my head, glancing at the mantel. There were pictures of his departed mother. Outside of that, he had no other pictures, no brothers or sisters. "His clan?"

Alexa slowly nodded. "We should check."

"Yeah…"

Resolved and somehow sadder than ever, we scooted out of the late dwarf's apartment. It was a sad thing, to die and have no one to take care of your pets. Or belongings. Or…

"Hey," I called, stopping Alexa as we walked to the elevator. "I'll be right back."

"What?"

I waved away Alexa's question while trying to recall if the kitchen had any garbage bags. Then I headed back to Shane's bedroom and sock cupboard. Some things… well, it was the right thing to do.

Chapter 6

We pulled up across the street from the White Scarves's meeting place, a non-descript double-story retail building with shuttered windows and a single wooden door on the outskirts of our two-block Chinatown. The building had a small, almost hidden sign reading the "White Scarf Chinese Cultural Association," the only thing denoting what lay within. Officially, Chinatown started a block away, though like most communities, the official Chinatown was really only comprised of overpriced restaurants, tourist shops, and a few grocery stores.

We sat and watched the building for a few minutes after Alexa parked, eyeballing the location and its various wards. Magic itself was like mathematics. Even if the symbols used to indicate the formula were unknown, they all had the same logic underlying the symbology. While it took me a bit of time to figure out the symbols, I worked them out.

"Nothing too unusual," I said. "Wards of reinforcement. Pest control. Ignorance. There's also an attack ward, but I can't tell what it does. Lots of lightning though."

Alexa grimaced but finally opened the door. Together we exited the car and headed for the building. After we knocked on the door for a bit, it was finally opened.

"Members only," the portly, mustached man inside snapped at us before he started closing the door.

"I'm here to speak with the White Scarves," I said, putting a hand on the door. Unfortunately, my actions did nothing to stop the door from continuing to swing close.

"No."

When the door was nearly closed, Alexa slapped her palm against it with a thump, putting the closing to a halt. She pushed, sending the man stumbling back.

"The Mage wants to speak with your people." So saying, she scooted past me and strode in, before freezing three steps in.

"Alexa?" I blinked as she stood frozen and I managed to squeeze past her. Only to see what had stopped her. "Oh."

A half dozen men sat around foldout circular tables, bottles of beer and bowls of sesame seeds spread before them. Each of the men was looking at us, the barrels of revolvers and pistols pointed directly at us.

The portly man sneered. "Members only."

"Yeah, no," I said, flicking my hand sideways. That was not the way I'd wanted to play it, but now that we were there, I wasn't going to let my friend be filled with lead. Power swelled as I formed but did not cast my Force Wall, ready to catch their bullets. Really, they should have just shot us if they intended to make use of those guns. "We're not here to cause trouble. We just have a few questions."

"Members—"

"Only. I got it. Look. You aren't going to shoot us. Especially not when your silencing wards are down."

"Our wards aren't—" The door warden's eyes widened as he saw the light show happening along the edge of the property. The wards weren't actually down, but as a mundane, he wouldn't know.

"So. Your bosses. Or we can just stand around all day," I said.

The door warden's lip curled up, and he walked to the staircase and ascended. He was gone for long minutes, minutes that we spent under the barrels of guns. Of course, I didn't waste that time, edging my body sideways so they couldn't see my fingers as I manipulated the spell forces, burning new linked wards around the building and beneath the concrete under our feet.

Force Ward Cast
Synchronicity: 86%

Disruptive Ward Cast
Synchronicity: 37%

Spell after spell, I layered defenses around their defenses. Layering protection around us. Just in case things went bad. It was how smart magicians worked, taking the time to set up a scenario they could win. I also, however, kept a close eye on how much Mana I had, knowing I'd need it if things went bad. You never really know how things would play out, which was why instant-cast spells like the ones I used were still preferred over wards and enchantments.

When the door warden finally made his way down, he looked entirely put out. A few gruff words of command later, guns were put away and we were escorted up the stairs. I had to admit my back itched the entire walk up, wondering if there was a hidden order to shoot us. It was only as I was nearly at the top of the staircase that one of the heretofore-silent men below spoke.

"Damn banana."

I stiffened, and Alexa, somehow sensing the change in my movement, looked back. I shook my head, dismissing her concerned look as I refocused on what was important. Like our coming meeting.

***

A simple reception area greets us when we make our way up, and then we're led past a board room to an office. Behind a brown desk featuring a monitor and one of those underpowered, overpriced mini-desktops sat a fifty-something Chinese man, his half-balding head of hair combed back where traces of grey appeared. He looked up from his keyboard, hidden behind paper and a trio of photograph stands.

Beside him stood another Chinese man. Unlike his officemate, he was larger, a man who obviously saw the inside of a gym on a semi-regular basis. Muscular, but with a layer of fat that appeared when one got older and lazier. The T-shirt denoting a boy band concert of some form stood in stark contrast to his large, intimidating demeanor. Powerful—in a mundane way. But mundane or not, he was armed with the highest variety and quality of enchanted equipment I'd seen. Everything from the bracers on his wrists and ankles to his necklace and hairband were enchanted. The knife in his boot and the gun on his hip were all powered too, and the shining pair of rectangles in his pockets told me that he'd probably enchanted the individual bullets in the gun.

"Mage Tsien. You came into our house, demanding answers. Why?" The seated man looked directly at me then flicked a dismissive glance at Alexa, who had stepped away to regard the enforcer.

"I'd be happy to answer your questions, but I'd also like to know who I'm talking to," I said.

"You can call me Manager Kim. And this is Brother Lu," Kim said.

"Okay. Firstly, thank you. I'm sorry we pushed in when we weren't meant to. We just have a question about Shane Travertine. He was supposed to visit you a few days ago."

"We heard of the attack on you. And his death. You think we had something to do with it?" Lu asked, his voice accusatory.

"No. I just need to know why he came," I said. "And what time he left."

"None of your business," Lu said.

Alexa shifted at his words, but I held up a hand, stopping her from moving.

"Look, I know it's none of our business what he did here. But you know he died, right?" When I received a nod from Kim, I continued. "Well, I want to find out why he died. Surely you don't begrudge him that."

"He's dead. Doesn't matter to him."

"I bet his ghost wouldn't say that," I said.

The pair exchanged glances, looking slightly worried. I wasn't surprised they were concerned. After all, ghosts were annoying. Few of them had the strength to do any real damage, but having one haunt you could be frustrating. And potentially dangerous, if you had a newborn. The reflection in the window that Lu sat with his back to showed the pictures of his new, happy family.

"He never seemed like one to haunt. And his clan will deal with him," Lu said, but I heard his trace of uncertainty.

"I just need a confirmation he arrived and when he left," I wheedled.

"Two p.m.," Kim said, shaking his head. When I moved to thank him and leave, he held up a hand, stopping me. "Why did you betray your people?"

"What?"

"You have chosen to be a… Mage," Kim almost spat the word, shaking his head. "Aligning yourself with the Western Imperialists. Why?"

"What are we, in a bad nineties Hong Kong film?"

My words made the pair glare. Alexa looked stern to anyone who didn't know her, but I saw her slight amusement at my words.

"You joke, but you betrayed your people. Learning rubbish magic from those who destroyed our very foundations. Why did you not join us?" Kim slapped his hand on the table. "Do you not care that they destroyed our people, weakened us so that we had to leave our motherland just to survive?"

"Not really."

How could I explain that what I learnt from Caleb was mainly magic theory, concepts and history rather than detailed casting. For the most part, I didn't even use sixty percent of what he taught. Sure, some of the fundamentals were useful, but the magic theory that Lily deposited in my brain was often more sophisticated and complex than anything I learnt from Caleb.

Even if I could explain that, I wouldn't. For the last twenty levels, I'd be dumbing down what I knew and cast so that I wasn't showing my entire range of knowledge to Caleb. As it was, I startled the Mage repeatedly with the way I combined spells. Or, more truthfully, the way Lily taught me to combine spells.

"I joined the Mages because they came to me and are teaching me," I said. "They offered protection and lessons. If you all came, well…"

"Well?"

"I might have chosen to learn from you. But I didn't even know you guys were here till now," I said flatly. "Which kind of tells me you aren't much of a power. In this city at least."

Lu shifted, a hand drifting toward the butt of his pistol. Alexa's eyes narrowed, though Lu's motion looked more an unconscious threat than a conscious one. Still, unconscious or not, it was a threat.

"We might not have much presence in this city, but we are still strong in Asia. You would do well to not underestimate us," Lu said.

"I'm not. Just stating a fact." And I meant it. It had taken Lily a bit to figure out how to classify Lu, but he was within range to be a threat for me. Being a mundane and having enchanted equipment meant he could theoretically end me without her interference.

Lu (Level 47—Human)
HP: 100/100
Mana: 0/0

Kim at least was in the tens, a normal human by Lily's standards. But as the Manager, the local boss, his danger was not in how hard he could hit but the number of people he could send to do the hitting. Because at the end of the day, no matter how much magic I wielded, I was still a squishy human underneath.

"And if you're threatening us, you might as well get in line," Alexa said, snorting at the pair.

"There is no line, Templar," Kim said scornfully. "If we want you dead, we will not hesitate. And your actions have driven many to seek such action."

"Actions?" I frowned, cocking my head. "Look, we've been rude here, but killing us seems a little much, no?"

"Not this. That… genie of yours. She is a danger. To all of us," Kim said, shaking his head. "Her presence is a danger. If we did not have our own artifacts, we would be concerned."

Faction Information: White Scarves

Formerly based in mainland China, emigrated to Taiwan, as did many other secret societies due to purges by their Socialist Republic of China. One of eleven major secret societies in Taiwan who control the majority of supernatural activity within the country. Has multiple branches worldwide, though none have the same strength as the main quarters. Known for using internal and external magic sources, based on misconceptions formed from Taoist and Legalist magical theory.

Known Artifacts: Yi's Bow and Arrows, the 24 Ocean Calming Pearls, the Golden Brick

I grunted as Lily finally updated their faction information. It was amusing, since most of that was knowledge I would never have gotten if not for the fact that she had decided that a Wikipedia entry of factions was part of the game experience. Their artifacts were all just powerful enchanted objects—able to level the playing field, but to call them a similar strength to my ring was a bit of an exaggeration. Still… a Golden Brick?

"Sure, sure," I said, deciding to give them face. "I can understand how Lily could be a concern. But she's not going anywhere, not for a while. But your warning is well taken."

"Lily." Lu snorts. "You really do like your white friends."

"First, Lily's a jinn. She's not white or brown or… whatever. Secondly, you're an ass," I said, glaring at him. "Lastly, I do like my friends." Turning on my heels, I walked to the door and nodded to Alexa. "Let's go."

I saw Kim try to say something, but I was incensed enough that I didn't stop. There was no point in talking to them anyway. I'd met enough racist asses on both ends of the spectrum. Some, having been beaten down enough, decided to play the victim card unceasingly. It was always worse when they hung out with their own, staying with others who shared their background, race, and views. Never trying to see a different viewpoint, never traveling. That process of creating silos created echo chambers of beliefs, reinforcing their belief that their hurt, their pain was more important than any others'. And it was true enough that we all justified our pain and playing the victim. But at a certain point, you just had to keep moving.

We only spoke once we were a distance away in the car. And more to focus on something else, something worth talking about.

"They know about Lily," I said. "They know people are coming after us."

"Picked that up. Sounds like it's not just one group, if they've picked that up too," Alexa said, her frown creasing. "I wonder how many."

"I don't know. But I think we know someone who might. And might be willing to tell us."

"You don't mean…"

"I do."

"You…" Alexa huffed then muttered something under her breath. Still, she took the next turn, heading away from the house.

At least we'd confirmed—at least we thought we had—that Shane had been alive when he left the Scarves. If the names of those after us were being bandied around so much, we might have another clue.

Chapter 7

Nora's hadn't changed. Even if I hadn't been back in a few months, the clothing store was the same. To mundane eyes, the used clothing store was filled with cheap, well-kept clothing brought there by thrifty individuals, dumpster divers, and locker clearers like I had been. The only incongruity were the wooden cupboards lining the walls, cupboards that were rarely opened when non-magical individuals were around. Simple "ignore me" wards along the cupboards ensured that no one paid attention to them. Of course, the wards were so low-powered that any supernatural and a few Gifted individuals would automatically ignore the spells. But that too was by design.

After all, El had to find customers for her real business somewhere. As the foremost material merchant in the city, El was both a great salesperson and collector. And while it was mostly Mages who made use of her services, she did dabble in other enchanted objects too. Or knew who would sell or trade them. Which meant she had a ton of connections throughout the city.

"El!" I waved to her after walking in, wrinkling my nose slightly as I noticed the incense. I let my eyes unfocus for a second to see what kind of glamour the pixie was using. The old matronly woman that I'd known before flashed into focus, along with her humdrum pink-and-green flowery dress, a piece of clothing that could have been taken right off her racks. Then I let my Mage Sight reassert itself and the redhead, pointed-long-eared pixie came into focus. "Got a moment?"

"Just doing inventory," El said, wrinkling her nose in such an adorable look that I wanted to say aww. "Stupid business is doing better."

"Huh?"

"The clothing business. I think there's going to be a recession again," El said, shaking her head. "Every time, we get more customers here before a recession. Means I go through inventory faster and have to buy more too. I need to hire again."

Drawn into the conversation, I went over to the counter where she was sorting clothes and leaned against it. "So do you hire supes because of your other business?"

"Of course. But you'd be surprised how hard it is to hire properly. Anyone with any ambition is always snapped up by others. Even if you find someone good, in a few years, they're gone. Either for a better job or… well."

Knowing El as I did, a lot of her hires probably came from the bad side of the tracks—orcs, goblins, and others who weren't trendy enough to be considered a "dark race" but who still suffered the consequences of not being passable as a human. Stuck living on the edges, many of them found legal work difficult, and so ended up dabbling in illegal or supernatural work. Neither of which was safe.

"Sorry to hear that."

"Forget sorry. Want a job?" she asked.

"No."

"Bah. Ever since you got your magic, you've gotten all kinds of posh." El sniffed, teasing me. She looked at Alexa, raising one elegant eyebrow at the blonde.

"No, thank you. I'm not very good at…" Alexa hunted for the right word.

"Fashion?" I added helpfully before yelping as she kicked me.

"Why are you here?" El said, turning the conversation back.

"Ah. Ummm… have you heard about Shane?" I said, lowering my voice.

When El indicated she hadn't, I winced and told her the story. In the silence that flowed through the store afterward, a pair of shoppers came in, chatting merrily as they browsed through the women's racks.

I eyed the girls, teenagers who had no clue what we had been speaking about, and dropped my voice a little. "Anyway. I was hoping you'd heard of people going after me."

"After you?" El shook her head. "There's been talk of your levels and Lily, but no one mentioned an attack. I'd have told you otherwise."

"Yeah… think you could look into it?" I offered her a smile, mocking myself as I did so. "We're out of leads right now. At least till someone tells us what's going on. But I'm not a fan of being a mushroom, you know?"

El nodded then straightened. "Oh hell. I got to deal with them."

Stomping off, the little pixie headed toward the pair of shoppers who'd gone extremely quiet. I cocked my head to the side, only to have my arm grabbed and myself pulled away.

"What?"

"Shoplifters."

"Oh." I sighed and let El deal with them.

Outside, Alex and I stared at one another, debating what next to do. It wasn't as if I had a clue.

As my stomach rumbled and the evening light slowly darkened, I sighed. "Let's go eat."

***

One of the advantages of visiting El was that we managed to swing by my favorite Greek restaurant, a place where they served both quantity and quality. The lamb shoulder was fall-off-the-bone succulent, and the rice was cooked just right, herbed and soaked in butter and the lamb juices by the time we made it home. I might have splurged, picking up both calamari and moussaka to share with Lily, along with her own dish of lamb. Alexa got a large Greek salad which she'd eat before stealing much more delicious food from the two of us. What could I say? We'd corrupted the woman.

Dinner was good, if subdued. As much as I liked to think I'd gotten people wanting me dead, having them actually act on it was another thing entirely. I'd mostly been putting the danger out of mind, figuring I'd seriously think about it when I hit Level 80 or so before. But it could be that my continued progression had triggered concerns about exactly how powerful I would be at Level 100.

I was packing up the leftovers when I asked the question that had been on all our minds. "What now?"

There was a deep and uncomfortable silence that stretched and stretched. No one had anything to offer. Should we just go back to normal? Should we keep knocking on doors, hoping something will give? Should I ask Caleb, our only source into our guardians, and hope he'd deign to tell us something?

"Well, we could…" Alexa opened her mouth, then seemed to change her mind. "I could ask my friends? In the Order."

"Are they still talking to you?" I said, eyebrow rising.

"A few, but they're not really connected to this. Most are, well, most are still training…"

Right, that made sense. Her friends would be Initiates like her, people she might have grown up with. Which meant they'd probably not know much, if anything.

"No. Not yet. I mean, they're unlikely to know anything, right?" Alexa nodded. "Let's table that for now. I'll bug Caleb tomorrow…"

I paused, a sense of pressure coming from the door. I was alerted before the door was knocked upon, the individual behind it so strong that his aura was like a physical thing.

When I looked at Lily, she smiled. "Don't worry. Well out of your Level."

I couldn't help but nod in gratitude. If she hadn't been smart enough to block off individuals of power from interacting with me directly, I'd have lost the ring—or my life—a long time ago. Even so, people had been finding ways around the entire thing, especially lately.

When I opened the door, staring back at me was a trio, each of which were as powerful, if not more so, than Caleb. The first was a small woman with greying, long brown hair, a flowery dress covering a bony body. She absently picked at the fraying edges of her dress's long sleeves when I opened the door, ignoring me entirely. She could be someone's mother, if not for my magic senses.

On the other hand, the big man standing at the forefront—presumably the one who had knocked on the door—could have just walked off a lumberyard. Red and black plaid shirt, big bushy beard, and thick, steel-toed shoes completed the ensemble as he glowered at me from nearly a foot over my head. I had to admit, I stepped back just from the suffocating physical presence he exuded.

As the last member of the trio, the Native American man looked the most normal. Clad in a simple shirt and jean ensemble, he had a green windbreaker over his torso and hands stuck in his pockets. But as an indicator of his strength, the glow of the fetish around his neck was powerful enough to make me dial down my sensitivity. It was kind of like looking at a Third Circle Mage's staff in action. Just a little too much for a casual evening.

"Mr. Tsien, may we come in?" the man in front spoke, not giving me more time to review the group.

"Uhhh… who are you?" Not that I couldn't guess, not with all the hints, but always good to ask.

"I am Druid Osian Carr. This is Witch Milli Cook and Doctor Chunta David. We're part of a group of concerned individuals," Osian said.

"Doctor?" I frowned, looking at Chunta.

"Medical. I prefer to go by that," Chunta clarified.

Well, I would too if I'd spent half a million dollars for an education. Then again, he was old enough that maybe he'd had it cheaper. If not easier.

"Yeah, I guess." I stepped back and waved them in while Lily moved her computers out of the way.

As each of them passed through my wards, they set off a small light display, their sheer presence affecting my wards and straining them. My wards weren't badly made—they weren't great, but they weren't horrendous—but each of the visitors was the magical equivalent of a nuke. The sheer amount of energy they output, just by being, was enough to make my wards react.

"This is the jinn, is it?" Milli said as she walked into the living room, staring at Lily.

While the others might be taking in the room or our notes or Alexa casually leaning against the wall and her spear, Milli was solely focused on Lily. She stared at Lily with an intensity that she had not showcased before and was unconsciously stirring the ambient Mana and spiritual realms. I saw how my wards reacted as the spirits and ghosts the Witch, and probably seer, interacted with rose to do her unconscious bidding and were blocked.

"Yes." Lily tilted her head.

Suddenly, the light show around my wards stopped. The wards themselves were protected as Lily sent the spirits and ghosts running away. There was no ripple of power, no magical warning. She just looked and they ran.

"You're the one, aren't you?" Milli said, nodding then walking over to the most comfortable seat in the house—mine—and flopping down. "Do we get tea? I like tea. But none of that flowery stuff. Real tea."

I was a bit whipsawed by the change as both of the other extremely powerful personages took seats on my lounge, giving me drink orders. Rather than fight it, I got out the cookies, Cheetos, and other snacks from our last gaming day and drinks. Chunta was a cola drinker, while Osian had a beer.

He wrinkled his nose a bit at the beer we handed him, muttering something about worse than water, but I was more than content to ignore him. As if I could have afforded craft beer.

"So. What are the three founding members of the Pagan Circle doing in my living room?" I said when I was finally seated.

"Just two," Milli said, offering me a half-smile. "I was a late comer."

"Right, right. But—"

"We'd like to speak with you. And your jinn," Osian said, leaning forward and taking our attention with that small movement. "The attack on you was well coordinated. The follow-up nearly took us by surprise as well."

"Follow-up?" I squeaked.

"Yes. Another group tried to sneak close to your residence while we were paying attention to the initial attack. Luckily, Milli learnt of the matter and the suborned pair of Mages," Osian said, shaking his head. "We managed to deal with the matter, but it seems your enemies have grown more persistent."

"Must have been quiet," I said softly. "I never even noticed."

"A simple isolation spell." Except there was nothing simple about a spell that could conceal the equivalent of a magic battle right outside my door, no matter what Osian said. Even if it was possible, there was nothing simple about it. "But that—or our losses—was not what we came to talk to you about."

"Then what is?" I said, tilting my head.

"We are here to talk about your future," Osian said. "We assumed that when you … Level up, you would be independent. A free agent. You've shown, in the past, disdain toward authority and organizations. But recently, you and the Mage Council have been flouting your relationship."

I frowned. "Caleb's teaching me."

"And your upcoming graduation," Osian added. "Do you intend to join them?"

"I… well…" I leaned back, my mind spinning. Pieces that I hadn't really put into place found their place and I exhaled, swearing. "Of course. You all think I'm going to join them and give them Lily's ring."

"On your death, yes. Or worse, lend the jinn's magical knowledge to them." Osian took a sip of the beer and made a face, putting it down. "That's not a good thing, especially for us."

"Especially for you?"

"We"—a hand waved toward the three of them, but I knew it really meant their group—"are representatives of a group, a series of teachings that don't fit with your Mage Council. They might not think we're evil, but—"

"But they're the bigger organization and eventually they'll stamp you out?" I kind of knew what he was talking about. Caleb had a tendency to be arrogant, and the rest of his people were even worse. Much worse. "You're worried they'll keep drawing others away, draining you of your people? Eventually killing your traditions?"

"If I was teaching them, that'd be the best," Lily said, shaking her head. "Your magics, all of it, are so damn inefficient."

"Lily—"

"No. Let the jinn speak," Chunta said, fixing Lily with his gaze. "Let her tell us how we are failing."

"It's not a matter of failing. It's the fact that you are not very good at what you're doing," said Lily. "Oh, you might have picked up a few new tricks and maybe even made some progress, but the way you handle power is so inefficient. Your ancestors were doing better two hundred years ago."

"Are you blaming us for losing some of our knowledge?" Chunta growled.

"Blaming? Did I ever say blame? No. I just said you guys have lost much of the magic you had and are busy recreating it." Lily pointed at each of the three. "All of you have so much power, you set off Henry's sloppy wards."

"Hey!"

"And it's not even a case of you throwing your weight around. None of you can actually control your auras." Lily sniffed disparagingly. "All of you, from Mages to Druids, you're so busy fighting over whose magic is better, whose magic is more correct or more traditional, that you ignore what's best. Mer, Yup'ik, Solomon, none of them would ever have been so sloppy. Magic is about will and training. It's about formula, vision, and practice. And all of you guys, you keep thinking that your way is the best. But the best, the smartest, the most powerful—they stole and used and adjusted from every tradition.

"So, yeah. If I was teaching them, the Mage Council would steal your 'people' and they'd be best. Because I'd teach them how to do real magic, not the party tricks you're so proud of."

"I told you. She's a demon," Chunta said, leaning back, his earlier anger gone as he looked at his friends. For a man who had angered and set off Lily's rant, he seemed entirely unconcerned about her. "She cares nothing for our people or our traditions. It is best that she is destroyed."

"I do not agree," Osian said, shaking his head. "While she might be blunt, she's correct that we all have lost much knowledge. If she—if Henry—is willing to teach us some of our old magic—"

"Bah, the boy has already been corrupted by her and the Council," Chunta said. "Too much danger. Let them die."

"Hey!" I said, rapping my fingers on the table. "We're right here, you know."

"Deciding their fate was not what we were charged with by the Circle. We are here to investigate," Osian continued to speak to Chunta, ignoring me.

In her seat, sipping on her cup of steaming tea and seeming above it all, Milli stayed silent as the boys argued.

"I said, I'm right here," I said, rapping the table harder. "So why don't you guys try talking to me rather than making guesses?"

And then I got my wish, as both of them turned to regard me. My throat went dry as they looked at me as if expecting me to speak.

I struggled for a second and cleared my throat before I spoke. "Look. I don't know about tradition or what magic is better. Well, I do, sort of. Because Lily is right. She teaches magic, pure magic. I've got… information, spells, data rattling around my head. And sometimes what I learn from the Mages isn't right, and what I have works better.

"And yeah, I'm taking their apprentice test. But that's because they offered to let me take it. Offered to teach me." I drew a deep breath and plunged on, not entirely sure where I was going with this, but knowing that I needed to finish talking before they decided to interrupt me. "And you guys never did. You just watched over me, thinking somehow I'd join you guys for some reason? Hell, I never even talked to you or your guardians. As far as I could tell, you guys wanted me dead as much as the Templars did.

"So maybe I figured the Mage Council was my only choice because they were the only ones to offer another option. Now that you're actually talking to me, well, things have changed, no? And maybe we'll be able to talk about different choices. But even if there isn't, why does everyone think I'm going to go lockstep with the Council? They're a bunch of arrogant asses."

I ran out of breath and grabbed my cup, draining it to fill my dry mouth and to find something, anything to do. When I set down my cup, the trio were sharing looks between one another before standing.

"What?" I said.

"I believe we've learnt all we needed to," Osian said.

Chunta snorted at me, striding to the door, not even waiting for his companions to catch up. Alexa watched over the group as they left—a little more politely in the other two's cases, but just as quickly. In short order, the three of us were alone once again.

After I flopped onto the couch with a newly retrieved can of pop, I placed it on my head and groaned softly. "I screwed up, didn't I?"

"I'm not sure there was anything you could ever do," Alexa said, letting the window blinds she'd been peering out of close.

"Osian and Milli looked to be open to changing their minds—"

"Milli was here to see me," Lily said. "I don't think whatever you did or said made a difference. Once she gauged my strength, she'd made up her mind."

"How…" I clamped my lips shut. I wasn't sure I agreed with her evaluation. Certainly, I didn't see anything that Milli had done that warranted that belief. "But is it because I'm getting close to the Mages? Is that the reason for all this?"

Alexa shrugged. "Maybe. Or it could be a good excuse. It could be that the deals are done, that the balance of those wanting you dead has tipped."

I sighed plaintively. "Hopefully they'll reconsider. Maybe, maybe they'll even help."

Alexa looked at me pityingly but eventually relented. "Maybe."

Chapter 8

"Fancy seeing you here this early," I greeted Caleb, my sort-of teacher. And it was early—we'd barely started breakfast before the knocking on the door.

"What did you say to the pagans?" Caleb snapped, pushing his way in.

I sighed again. One of the aspects of my wards were that I'd keyed them to allow in those with no hostile intent. While it'd be simple enough for someone at Caleb's level to spoof the spell, he—like our earlier visitors—was still limited by Lily. And anyone at my strength level would find it hard to beat my wards.

"What happened?" I said, growing serious. I saw how agitated the Mage was in the way he looked at me, the way he stomped past me, barely even glancing at Lily or Alexa in their morning clothes. Which was a bit of a sight since Lily was in a pink bunny onesie and Alexa was already dressed for her morning exercises.

"They withdrew their support this morning," Caleb said, lips pursing. "As did two-thirds of those watching over you. Even the Templars have indicated that the Orders are in discussion if they should continue to support us."

"Wait. What? I thought they wanted the ring…" I looked at Alexa. I wasn't entirely sure why they wanted the ring. They'd never really explained it.

At my look, Alexa shrugged.

"They did. But they're not as large as they used to be, and there are concerns that losing more people to protect, well, you isn't worth it." Caleb's eyes narrowed as he continued. "I've been called back to speak to the Council itself. On the same topic."

My jaw dropped. "Are you guys abandoning me too?"

"No. Not if I have anything to say about it," Caleb stated. "But some assurances would be reassuring."

"Assurances on what?"

"That you'll join us. That when you're done with the ring, you'll pass it on to our safekeeping." Caleb raised a finger. "No matter what they say of us, we are good at keeping the really bad artifacts out of circulation."

"Bad artifacts?"

"Yes. Like Blackbeard's Chest. Muhammad's Pot. The Strangling Rope of Kuching."

"Never heard of them."

"Exactly!"

Rather than reply to Caleb, I looked at Lily, who shrugged. "He's not wrong. The Mage Council's Vault of Unending Space is well-known to be very secure."

I gave Lily a curt nod before looking at Caleb, muttering to stall for time as my mind swirled, "You know that the reason we're getting so much pushback is because the Mage Council is trying to take it all. Everyone's worried that I'm tilting too much in your favor. That it isn't going to be a fair competition in the end and you guys are all going to pile on."

Caleb shrugged. "Lily's knowledge is certainly a draw for us. As is the ring and the powers it holds. But understand, we're as interested in you. Despite your unorthodox introduction to our world, you've adapted well. Your magic—your spells—give you an unprecedented flexibility, especially compared to our own apprentices. Already we're adjusting the lessons we provide from our reports. I expect great things from you. As do many on the Council."

I noted how Caleb was avoiding the point I was trying to make, trying to butter me up. Not that it didn't help. The usual taciturn Mage was actually complimenting me, which was a nice change. But… "I don't know. You're pretty nice, but I'm not sure I'd want to be made part of your Council. I barely know them."

"Then meet us."

I shook my head. "Not yet."

Caleb's eyes narrowed. "If you don't provide us any reassurance, trying to convince the Council to dedicate more resources will be difficult. At best. We might even be forced to back off."

"I know."

Caleb stared at me, letting his gaze do all the talking. But I refused to turn away from him or change my mind, and in the end, Caleb walked out, tutting to himself. I stayed serious till he was gone, then I broke into laughter as Lily mimicked Caleb's last moments, tutting and tapping her foot, arms beneath her breasts.

"Stop. Please," I said.

"But I'm so disappointed in you," Lily whined in a gruffer voice.

Alexa giggled, covering her mouth, and I laughed. For a time, we shared a laugh, then we turned to our food. Only when we were done and cleaning up did we turn our thoughts to our visit.

"Are you sure you don't want to meet the Council?" Alexa said, cocking her head.

"Mostly. They're… dangerous," I said. "Even if Lily can kick any one of their asses—"

"Or all of them!"

Ignoring Lily, I continued. "Going into their place of power would put even her at a disadvantage. They've had hundreds of years to layer defenses. I'm not sure even she could stop them from killing me if they wanted to."

"Right…" Alexa cocked her head to the side. "Sorry, I'm just used to Lily being, well, Lily."

"She's powerful, but not omnipotent," I said. "Until I can escape by myself, I won't put myself in such a situation."

"But we're going to lose all our support." Alexa looked at the door and what lay behind. "Do you think the government…?"

"They'll stay out of it." After placing the dish in the drying rack with the rest of the plates, I wiped my hands dry and stepped away from the sink. "That's their modus operandi, no? They leave us to deal with one another, while keeping an eye that things don't get out of hand. It's too much trouble to get rid of us, especially when the supernatural world is slowly dying out."

Alexa made a face but had to agree. As powerful as magic was, as powerful as we were individually, humanity had the numbers and the technology to more than even the odds. It was why the supernatural world lived peacefully alongside humanity. For the most part. There were still a few countries run by supernaturals, but it was often in the background, as puppeteers rather than the face.

"Then what do we do?" Alexa said as she poured herself another cup of coffee.

"Well, the Mages and the Order haven't left yet. So I figure we should look at what we can do to upgrade our defenses," I said, looking around our house, eyeing the now-quiet wards. To make sure we didn't have to pay the damage deposit, when I created the wards, I'd actually painted them on using a metallic paint. Where I could, on particularly worrisome areas—like our front door and the frame—I'd carved into the wood itself. But for the most part, the wards were anchored by paint and Mana, which I had to admit was not the most powerful method. "For that, we'll need more—"

"Money." Alexa nodded. "I'll go find some quests then."

I nodded, walking over to my computer. Time to check the good old job board.

***

It was interesting how more and more work had transferred over to the job board in the last couple of years. At first, only edge cases and those desperate for trivial help posted on the board. But as people got used to it, more and more jobs were posted. It helped that Bast, the board owner, had upgraded functionality and now, everyone who used the board had their own profile. Jobs were graded according to their difficulty, and those looking to take the jobs were also graded on their profile as they completed each job publicly.

To keep up with the growth of the job postings, Bast had even taken to outsourcing the work, with each local region having their own moderators who reviewed profiles, made sure no one doubled-up on profiles, and that all jobs were appropriately categorized. The last was probably the biggest concern, since a badly categorized job could lead to harm or a failure due to no fault of the job-taker. It was why ratings had been created for both sides.

The last reason the job board was popular was due to the fact that all high-tier jobs were verified by Bast herself, which made taking those jobs much less risky. Of course, to get the right to do those jobs—or post them—the various groups had to work themselves up, ensuring a high clear rate on the board.

All of which meant I had a chance to view the wide variety of jobs now available for someone like me. It was part of why El didn't see me that much anymore, since I was rather busy. This time around though, I changed my filter settings.

Normally, I filtered for complex, decently paying jobs with no violence involved. Since I wasn't a traditional RPG character, I didn't need to kill things to Level up. And while combat would increase my Level, it was only because I was getting better at casting spells under duress—combining knowledge that had been inserted into my brain with the knowledge that I'd learned and teased apart in my studies. It wasn't because I was getting some weird "experience" from fighting.

As such, I generally avoided violent missions. Of course, as one of the stronger supernaturals in town—at least, stronger freelancing supernaturals—I often ended up dealing with the really nasty problems anyway. But most of those were by personal request rather than choice.

Today was different.

Today, I looked for jobs that were high paying and could be completed in a day or less. Which, obviously, meant no gathering jobs, no ward reinforcement or enchantment fixing, no alchemical potions needing to be brewed or artist's show being developed. No. It meant dealing with the kind of things that the sane didn't want to deal with.

A supernatural fungal infestation in an alchemist warehouse that had grown semi-sentient and carnivorous.

An escaped chimera.

A new gang of redcaps making their presence known in the south west, mostly preying on teenagers by selling the latest drug.

Reports of a shadow creature moving in and out of bedrooms in a local neighborhood. Leaving behind the occasional smothered corpse and a lot of nightmares.

There were other reports, but these were the best paying. Over the next few hours, I reviewed information about each job. Just because a job was generally correct in its initial description did not mean that the details didn't paint a different picture.

The fungal infestation post had been up for three months, with two others having attempted to clear the infection. Initially, the in-house alchemist had come up with a potion to destroy the fungus and it had worked. Except for a small, unnoticed portion that had escaped the cleansing. When the fungus came back, it was resistant to the alchemical potion and the two other potions the in-house alchemist came up with. By that point, the warehouse had to be abandoned and the job put up. The first applicant to try to cleanse the warehouse was a shaman who'd brought numerous spirits to play, destroying the spiritual nexus of the fungus. Of course, that didn't work that well—for one thing, the spiritual body of a fungus was both nearly non-existent by nature and also quite hardy. The fungus had, once again, managed to escape total destruction. The next job-seeker was actually a group of sentient slimes who'd scoured the entire location. Until the fungus, having mutated again, drove the slimes away by destroying half of them.

"So. Carnivorous, semi-sentient, able to fight off slimes. And the job is rated a high C." I snorted in amusement. It might have started as a simple D rank problem, but by now, the job was approaching Bast level of attention. "Not touching this one with a ten-foot pole. Especially since the damn company still wants their goods 'intact.'"

Next up was the redcaps. A quick review of the job had me steering clear. Among other things, it looked like the reason why it was paying so much was because the local neighborhood supes had spotted a lot more mundane heat. Considering my current problems, getting entangled in a sting operation wasn't a good idea. Better to let that play out.

The shadow creature, on the other hand, was a nighttime problem. It was also inconsistent, which meant I'd need to access the homes of people who might—or might not—believe I was there to help, set up wards, and try to track the creature. If I was lucky, there was enough of a signature for that to happen. More likely, I'd be forced to set up large scale tracking wards and hope to catch it. Either way, not a quick solution. Which meant it shouldn't have been categorised as a 'quick' job. The joy of job hunting – no one ever categorised things properly.

That left the most dangerous—a solid C+ bordering on B—quest. Killing the chimera. The good news was, it had everything I needed—its lair was known, the payment was in an escrow account already, and I only needed to kill it because the chimera had gone feral. The bad news was that it was a chimera, which meant my magic would be less than useful due to its natural resistances.

"Alexa. Chimera?"

The blonde blinked, absently drying her hair after her shower. "Are you asking what they are or if we should fight one?"

"Fight. There's a quest for it."

"I'll have to do most of the work…" Alexa grinned. "Like usual."

"Funny. Let's get ready. And bring your net."

***

The chimera had gone to ground close by where it had escaped—in High Park, a small oasis of greenery in our urban jungle. The park was popular among joggers and hikers since it consisted of a trio of rolling hills with a jogging track circling the lower areas of the hills and rising over them occasionally. It was a good three mile workout if you ran the entire park, and I'd been there a couple of times during the summer months with Alexa.

Inside the park, off the main path, were dirt trails, kept in condition for those looking for more of a challenge and a greener run. I had to admit I much preferred jogging on the paths. The lack of tripping hazards and cobwebs to the face made me happy.

Alexa, on the other hand, was perfectly at ease walking on the dirt trails, her spear shaft used as a walking stick as we made our way deeper into the woods. We walked forward in silence, keeping an eye out for potential trouble, even if the job posting had indicated the chimera was lying low for the moment.

By the time we left the well-trod path, signs of the chimera's presence were making themselves known. First and foremost was the lack of noise. Not that the park was that noisy, but the occasional bird call, the scamper of a squirrel, or the buzzing of insects was gone entirely. None of them wanted anything to do with the chimera.

Next was the smell. It started out subtle, a hint of wet dog, and grew until it almost choked me with its intensity. That the smell was as much in my mind from the corrupted Mana the creature exuded did little for my gag reflex. Still, at least we knew we were on the right track.

"Net?" I said, gesturing to Alexa.

The blonde nodded and pulled off her bag, getting her equipment ready. I unslung my bag from both shoulders too, pulling the zipper wide but not reaching for any of my warding blocks. We'd discussed our optimal strategy on the drive over, and now, we needed to get close to verify its presence.

As a magical construct, chimeras had a few notable characteristics that made them difficult opponents for Mages. They were highly resistant to any magic cast on and at them. Even a spell like Mana bolt or fire bolt would find its effectiveness greatly reduced as the miasmic Mana the chimera exuded corrupted and broke down the spell forms. Closer to the chimera's body, the bolt would deflect or shift away, the power within dispersing. In some cases, chimeras were known to even gain strength from magic wielded against it. The most effective means of dealing with a chimera was via overwhelming force, using elemental bolts or force pushes and releasing the spells just before hitting the creature.

Because of the corruption and miasma and because of the chimera's original magic nature, scrying and tracking spells were of little use. The delicate spell forms broke down in short order around the creature or places it lived, and would alert the monster of our presence. Add in the fact that doing so would allow it to taste the "flavor" of my magic, and checking up on it magically was contraindicated.

The other aspect of chimeras that made them difficult to deal with were the sheer variety. The common image of a lion, goat, and dragon-headed creature was not wrong, just incomplete. Chimeras were magical constructs formed from multiple creatures smooshed together. The results were as varied as the insane mages and "scientists" who put them together. There was a small but healthy industry of "branded" chimeras—formulations of creatures that were sold as pets and guard dogs. In this case, we were facing one of the latter, its control spells damaged beyond repair after an "incident."

No. I didn't know what the incident was. And I hadn't asked.

Once Alexa was ready, wearing her armored coat and a scalemail skirt that ended just above her armored knees, we crept closer. The ex-Initiate had screwed on her spearhead and carried the weighted net in hand, gently pushing aside foliage with the tip of her spear.

As I ducked under a branch and grimaced as an unseen cobweb swept over my face, I spotted the hole the chimera had made its lair. A small mound of dirt fronted the hole that went under a fallen tree, the insides of the lair dark and uninviting. I held up my hand and pointed at Alexa, who nodded, both of us crouching a little to stay hidden. Seeing no movement, I frowned, debating our options.

If the chimera had left its lair, placing wards was a waste of time and could allow it to catch us. On the other hand, if it was in there, a series of wards were the safest way to capture it. On the third, non-existent hand, as I glanced at the darkened spots on the leaves around the lair, if the creature was out hunting, people were in danger.

I looked at Alexa, who lifted her net, gesturing toward the lair. I nodded, deciding to stick to our tentative plan. We split apart slightly, doing our best to sneak toward the lair. Unfortunately, I was paying too much attention to the lair itself and not enough to my footing. I stepped on a dry branch, sending a resounding crack through the still forest.

I froze. Alexa didn't as she rushed forward, swirling the net to make it open slightly. As I tensed, waiting for the creature to jump out, Alexa skidded to a stop near the exit. She paused, peering into the darkness before turning toward me, already shaking her head. I sighed, relaxing, and saw her eyes widen in shock.

Instinct from long years of practice had me throwing myself forward even as I formed the spell for a Force Wall. But as the spell formula rose in my mind, it felt slippery, twisty, refusing to come together with the same fluidity I was used to.

The chimera hit my upper back, making my graceful roll turn into a sprawl that jarred my head and left me with the taste of dirt and leaves in my mouth. The chimera was heavier than I'd expected, the ursine-canine mixture adding muscle and bone mass to the monster. Thankfully, the spelled duster kept it from doing any real damage, even as I desperately rolled to the side.

Force Wall Cast
Synchronicity: 31%

I splayed my fingers in front of my face, the Force Wall catching the slavering chimera just before it tore into my face. For the first time, I caught sight of the monster clearly. Wide jaws. A pair of extra-long canines on both the upper and lower levels of its teeth. A short tongue dripping frothy saliva. Two angry, tiny eyes stared at me as it snapped at the Force Wall again. Somehow, between my turn and the chimera adjusting its body for balance, I had managed to squirm it half-off me, its long and low-slung black-furred body resting only half on top of me. Even so, I felt the enchantments on my jacket activate as it pushed against the weight.

As I squirmed to get away and held it off with the Force Wall, I felt the spell formula squirm and twist, refusing to hold still as the chimera's essence ate away at my spell. A sharp pain and another hit my legs, like a hard stick slamming into them that left a stinging sensation behind. The attacks made the spell wobble as my concentration slipped. As I glanced down, I noted the trio of tails—each long and muscled, like a snake's body—and the way they whipped at my feet. If not for the enchantments I'd sewn into my jeans, I would have severely bruised thighs and calves. Or worse.

Another lunging snap caught only by me shrinking the size of the Force Wall again. The attack rebounded the chimera's face, smooshing its snout flat before it raised its head for another attack. Only to have a spear catch it in its upper body, thrown by my brawny friend. The spear took the creature just behind its foreleg, throwing it off me through sheer momentum and allowing me to roll away.

Alexa pounded over to me, already waving her net above her head as I came up to my knees. A languid toss of the net caught the back of the creature's body and part of the haft of her spear. The chimera squirmed away, getting to its feet and shaking its body to dislodge the spear and net. Too bad for it, it was my turn.

"Bog ground," I snapped and pointed down, my fingers flicking and twisting before splaying.

Multi-Linked Spell Bog Ground Cast
Synchronicity: 64%

The spell took effect, conjured elemental water filling the ground beneath the monster. At the same time, the viscosity of the ground decreased, sinking the chimera. It struggled, which made it sink faster. I didn't try to hold the spell together, sending a surge of Mana into the container before releasing it to begin my next spell.

Bog Ground was actually a multi-linked spell, one that linked Summon, Alter Temperature, Force Fingers, and Decrease Resistance together. Because of that, the complicated spell began to break down the moment I released it.

Next up, I formed an Ice Spear and threw it at the monster. The Bog Ground spell had dispersed, leaving the ground dry and hard and the chimera knee deep. The shard of ice slammed into the chimera's chest as it struggled free, throwing it backward. Hopping over, machete in hand, Alexa threw a cut that lopped off an ear, making the chimera howl once again.

With it trapped, injured, and surrounded, the rest of the fight was never in doubt.

***

Cleanse was such a powerful and useful spell. As I cleaned away traces of the fight and the blood on us, Alexa looked at the remnants of the chimera. She wrinkled her nose as the body parts continued their accelerated decay, leaving behind a ghastly smell and patches of meat and innards.

"Do we need to bring anything back?" Alexa said, looking entirely unimpressed with the thought of poking her fingers into that mess.

"Nah. We should be good. If there're concerns, they'll scry the location."

Nodding, Alexa finished cleaning her blade and waved me on. Together, we headed back for the car while I mentally spent our rewards. Getting sorted would be expensive.

Chapter 9

"Easy come, easy go," I muttered, staring at the handful of change I had left.

Splayed around the living room were the purchases I'd made, the vast majority coming from El, while the remainder had been picked up at the local hardware store. After some consideration, we'd decided against reinforcing the wards in-house. The time cost involved in developing thicker and more powerful wards was too high.

Rather than do that, I had chosen to work on a portable safeguard. That was why our coffee table had been pushed aside and the beginning of our warding circle rolled out on the floor. For the base, I'd decided to go with leather—specifically troll leather. The material had been carefully cured and still kept a little of its regenerative properties, allowing it to keep its pristine condition.

Having finished contemplating my poverty once again, I turned back to the leather. I was using a beam compass to draw out the edges of the circle on a giant sheet of paper pinned to the leather itself. Once I'd drawn the various runes in pencil, making sure I had enough space for everything, I would then have to enchant the entire thing.

Unlike most of my other wards, the portable shelter would be a short-lived defense. It wasn't meant to last forever. In fact, with the amount of power I intended to pump through the thing, I figured it'd burn out within five minutes even if no one attacked it. But those five minutes would allow the secondary enchantments to kick in.

Of course, before I could make the secondary enchantments, I needed to make sure the primary ones worked. Around me were the discarded pieces of paper from previous attempts. Each time, a minor mistake—or a better idea—spoiled my work. As I finished with the compass, I leaned back and sighed in relief. Step one, done.

"You know, this is the second day you've been at this," Alexa said, shaking her head as she leaned against the wall. "And you wanted to build more weapons, right?"

"I do. But this is more important," I said, pointing at the leather. "As you know, defensive enchantments are always stronger if they're pre-laid. I can cook up a powerful spell without a thought, but a properly enchanted circle could eat any attack of mine and laugh. It's why all-out attacks against a Mage's Tower were so rare. Anyway, I'll be done soon."

"You haven't even started inscribing the runes."

"But I've worked out what I want. Did you get the rest of my stuff?"

"Yes. Crushed deathwatch beetles, the extracted poison of a naga, and the lymph glands of a Chupacabra," Alexa said, wrinkling her nose.

"Great. I wrote the instructions somewhere…" I cast around, moving papers till I found the necessary document and waved it at the blonde. "Here. Follow instructions."

"I—"

"Lily!" I waited for the jinn to acknowledge my call before going on. "Can you watch Alexa and warn her if she does something wrong?"

Lily made her way down the stairs, her face furrowed with concentration. I waited while she tested the restrictions on her ring and the wish before she grimaced. "Yeah. I think so."

"See. Easy!" I cheerfully exclaimed to Alexa, who made a face at me.

I laughed, having passed on the most time consuming and smelly job. Of course, I could do it myself—and often did—but as Alexa had pointed out, we were short on time. Better to finish this now than to wait.

***

Staring at the slowly drying piece of enchanted leather, I eyed the magic circle critically in the waning light of evening. Not that the living room was dark—in fact, it was brighter than day with all the lights I had turned on. The various enchanted materials we'd mixed had been added to gold and silver dust before I had taken the time to carefully inscribe the entire thing. Rather than waste time painting it on, I'd used magic to keep the mixture melted and stirred while Force Fingers carefully guided the slow-flowing mixture in the correct paths. All the while, I infused the mixture with my

Mana and enscribed the runes with the spell formula.

The process had drained me more than any other enchantment I'd ever done and had taken the better part of four painstaking hours. The final result, to my eye, was perfect. Unfortunately, to the jinn's exacting nature, it was less so.

Enscribed Runic Portable Abode Cast
Spell Fidelity: 87.4%
Enchantment Durability: 34%
Max Duration: 6.7 minutes

Portable Abode
This portable abode is a travesty of magic and intent. Rather than building a permanent safe location, this abode focuses on thickening the defensive walls of the abode, ensuring that it can withstand a strike even by an Archmage. Or so the creator thinks. Currently, this is an incomplete enchantment with a loss of 5.8% efficiency due to unfinished connections in the center. Creates a 5' x 5' x 8' protected location when triggered.

"Harsh," I said, eyeing Lily.

"But fair." Lily shook her head. "I would have preferred something more traditional. But I understand your thinking."

I nodded. The second enchantment, the one I'd yet to complete, was a teleportation enchantment. It was basically a Linked enchantment with a spatial component. The goal was simple—you stepped into the circle, triggered the abode, and the protective walls came up. In the meantime, the teleportation enchantment made the connection to your teleportation location before sending you over.

The reason why I'd built it to last five minutes—rather than just a simple teleportation circle—was because teleportation was an incredibly complex spell. In fact, it was so complex that I couldn't actually do it. Not real teleportation.

So instead, I was going to cheat. The plan was to use Link, Anchor, and Summon spells to sidestep the concept of teleportation. Rather, I'd Summon us to the new location, with the individuals within the circle taking a short ride through another dimension. Much, much safer than an actual teleportation spell.

Still insanely dangerous, but much safer.

"Now that you've completed that perversion, what's your next plan?" Lily said, looking at the trio of plastic tubes I had resting to one side.

"Oh. Those. One-off-use wands," I said, grinning. "Except I've got this idea that rather than generate the air itself, if I use hollow plastic, I could just put a Gust spell within."

Lily's eyes narrowed in thought, but before she could hint at what I was doing wrong, a knock on our door drew us away. It was just the two of us, since Alexa was at her night job.

"Trouble?" I said, wandering over to the door while grabbing my staff. I'd leave it out of sight, behind the door, but I'd grown a little paranoid over the last few days.

"It normally doesn't knock," Lily pointed out.

"Huh. True." I opened the door.

Outside, to my surprise, a bike messenger stood, his hand raised to knock again. "Mr. Henry Tsien?"

"Yes?"

"Document for you." The messenger handed me a clipboard to sign before he relinquished the simple envelope.

"Thanks."

I was closing the door before I realized the poor fellow expected a tip. Unfortunately, I didn't have my wallet on me. Magical staff, sure. But wallet, no. Shaking my head, I closed the door fully and walked back to Lily, eyeing the purple envelope. For a small envelope, it had a certain heft and stiffness that spoke of high quality, thick paper. An invitation—old school too, with a seal on the back.

"Weird." I waved the paper in front of Lily's face.

When the jinn saw the seal on the back, she stiffened. The seal was dark red, a slight smear of color running and, as I raised the envelope further, gave off the slightest tingle of magic. Not enough for me to worry about a magical attack, though there was definitely magic in play here.

"Do you recognize it?"

Rather than answer directly, Lily nodded stiffly. When I realized I wasn't going to receive any further information from the jinn, I walked over to the kitchen counter and carefully set aside the mail. I grabbed my bag, pulled out my modifiable warding tablets, and flicked them around until I had the enchanted runes ready. Once I'd placed the envelope within my bag, I released a surge of power into the warding tablet and sealed the envelope away.

Once that was done, I focused and cast Force Fingers, manipulating the envelope to open it. As I broke the seal, a flicker of power escaped, rotating around as the notification spell hit the edges of my barrier and then, unable to escape, self-destructed. My eyes narrowed before I pulled out the card within.

The invitation was on fine purple paper, the note within written in a cursive script reminiscent of medieval Bibles rather than the functional cursive we'd been taught. I cocked my head, deciphering the words before turning the card around to check for a post-script. Finding nothing on the back or in the envelope, I released the Force Fingers spell while leaving the envelope trapped.

"How interesting," I muttered. "I didn't realize Rihanna was a magic user."

"*Rhiannon*! You ignorant, pop-culture-loving nerd! Rhiannon. The fae goddess!" Lily gave up on being quiet, only to clamp her mouth shut when she saw my crinkled eyes and choking laughter. Once I'd managed to get a hold of myself, she continued. "It's not a laughing matter. She's the queen of the fae. You can't turn down that invitation."

I cocked my head as I sobered up and pointed at Lily. "How powerful, exactly, is she?"

"Individually?" Lily played with a strand of hair as she walked away, tapping a few buttons to continue mining with her ship before she answered, her voice soft. "We don't count things that way. Didn't. Once you hit a certain… point, it's hard to really compare. Powerful enough, Henry. That should be enough for you."

I grunted, tapping the envelope again. "And why is she inviting me? Us?"

Lily shrugged, not offering an answer. Or perhaps unable to.

In either case, I looked at the invitation and waved at it. "So I'm assuming that's safe?"

When I got no answer from Lily, I sighed and pumped a little more Mana into the shield. Better to be safe than sorry then. I had the address memorized at least. Grabbing a pad, I scribbled a note for Alexa then got dressed. Considering the invitation requested an audience ASAP and Lily's reaction, letting them wait was a bad idea.

***

There were many places I'd expect to find a portal to Faery. A standing stone circle on a mist-enshrouded hilltop. Perhaps, if you were a Tolkien fan, the elves might be watching the opera or theatre—you know, refined and snooty. I would even accept a park or a secure warehouse, one that allowed large movements of people without issue—especially if they lay in a confluence of ley lines.

What I did not expect was for it to be inside a comedy club. Getting in was easy. All I had to do was pay the very reasonable door charge. That I was getting in toward the last half of the show meant that the door person was willing to give me a discount too. Inside, I headed to the bar opposite the stage, eyeing the dimly lit, half-filled room. I wrinkled my nose slightly as the smell of stale popcorn and alcohol mixed with the raucous laughter.

I ordered a beer and leaned against the bar. So. This was the address. And I assumed if I flashed the invitation, I'd have been led where I needed to go. But without it, I needed to work out by myself where I had to go. As I chuckled appreciatively at a joke about a chicken, a boat, and a college party, I let my Mana Sight activate.

It was always in play, to some extent. A Mage's ability to cut through most glamours, to sense Mana was always on. But there was a difference between looking and seeing—a shift of perception and attention. I stopped just looking and actually saw, letting the swirl of ambient Mana register in my consciousness. In short order, I chugged down half of the bottle, fortifying myself with some alcoholic courage, and headed for the washroom.

Pity I'd miss the rest of the act. But needs must when the fae called.

I made it most of the way down the corridor, bypassing the washrooms and heading for the "employee only" entrance before I was caught. The bouncer seemed to materialize from nowhere, his seven-foot, linebacker body form drawing my attention only when he leaned forward and put a meaty paw in my way.

"Employees only," he growled, his voice resounding in my chest like a rising drumroll.

Now that he'd moved, I could see him properly for what he was—a troll. A fae troll, not the German ones which are called the same but are an entirely different species. These guys are big, big eared and nosed, with magic in their blood and the strength of the mountains in their bones. In other words, he could have squashed me if he'd grabbed me.

"I'm invited," I said and held up a hand, letting a light spell form around my hand.

The troll watched my hand. "Mage Tsien."

Statement more than question, but I nodded. The troll dropped his hand, letting me by, and I walked to the door. A push let me in, leading down a corridor that shimmered before my eyes. I squinted slightly, realizing that the split in the corridor was both illusionary and true—one a magical road for those who could make it and another, the mundane route for the norms.

I exhaled, shaking my head at the casual use of magic. At the fact that the road to Faery wasn't a standing stone but an illusion in a comedy club. And because where I was going, I had never been before. As I stepped onto the road, a hand dropped onto my shoulder, forcing me to blink.

"Lily?" I gaped at my friend. "How…?"

"We are between and betwixt," Lily said. "Some rules are relaxed. And we were both invited, were we not?"

I was surprised by her presence, knowing how little Lily liked leaving the house. Even after all these years—which for the immortal jinn was probably an eyeblink—it was still uncommon for the jinn to voluntarily leave our house. Yet as we strode along the twisting cobblestone road, mist rising to brush against our legs, I found myself comforted by her presence.

"You do remember your stories about the fae, don't you?" Lily said, brushing dark hair back across her ears as she hunched in her favorite hoodie. It said "Let me show you true magic" with a book underneath.

"Yeah…" I scrambled through my memories. "They don't speak untruth, but they can lie via leading statements. Their promises are binding—as are mine. No eating food or drink, or taking gifts. Or offering them, because that'll create obligations."

Lily made a face, then waved. "Mostly. The first one is a lie, and the others have… refinements. But I don't have time to teach you court etiquette."

"Nor could you," I said, cocking my head.

Lily's shoulders rose in a nonchalant shrug. Out of conversation topics for the moment, I eyed our misty surroundings, devoid of sound the way only a mist-filled land could be. Everything, even my own steps, was muffled, while my ability to see had dropped from tens of feet to a few feet.

As we continued onward, I noticed how the mist was slowly growing less dense, more and more of the world becoming clear. Trees in the distance firmed up, their brown barks deepening even as their leaves danced on subtle wind. They shimmered, and I squinted, slowing down as I tried to grasp their meaning.

"Ooof." A hand grabbed mine and pulled my gaze away as Lily stumbled. I helped her regain her balance before she offered me a sheepish smile. "Loose stone."

"Oh…" I looked at the smooth cobblestones beneath my feet and then at the guileless jinn, before drawing a deep breath and setting my mental defenses higher. Even the trees were a danger here.

Because Faery was not part of Earth. Once, perhaps it had been, but now, it was a different land entirely. Much like Avalon, it existed in a parallel dimension, one reachable via such faery roads and circles, but separate and untouchable. It was a magical land, and as I walked, I sensed my magical senses, my sight, shivering and waking. The light here was brighter, the Mana more intense, the smells more potent. It was like taking a half dozen shots of energy drinks at one go, the way it made my body wake. I found myself smiling, even as I reached for the calm that I'd learned to exist in to cast magic.

An awning rose up from the hill without warning, the portable court blocking the light from the—two!—suns while those within lounged, laughed, and ate. The fae that stood in the tents were tall, reminiscent of Tolkien's elves but subtly different. Inhuman with sharp teeth and cunning eyes, while looking elegant and refined at the same time, clad in courtier clothing at least three centuries out of date. And in the center of the mobile court was a single chair where a woman lounged, clad not in courtier clothing but practical riding clothes. As I entered the tent, the group hushed.

For a moment, I froze, but subtle pressure on my arm that Lily had yet to release had me moving forward. I paused in front of the riding figure and bowed low. And then, catching Lily's beckoning hand beside me, went lower.

"Rise, Mage Tsien. It's a pleasure to see you too, Auntie." Rhiannon's voice was low, rough. Her accent was hard to place, her diction clear and distinct.

"Auntie?" I mouthed to Lily, who shushed me with her eyes and flicked her gaze back to the queen. Or god. Depending on who you asked.

"Thank you, Queen Rhiannon," I said, deciding on the lesser status. After all, she wasn't acting like a goddess to those present, but a queen at most. So I'd go with that. Also, it made my heart feel a lot better to deal with a supernatural fae queen rather than a goddess. "I received your kind invitation. Though—"

"You are wondering why I brought you here?"

"Yes, Your Majesty."

"We do not, normally, interact with the mortal world. Our time there has passed," Rhiannon said, her eyes twinkling slightly. "But you attracted our attention when you made inquiries about one of our former citizens."

"I did?" I blinked, then realization caught up. "The doppelganger."

"The Changeling," Rhiannon corrected gently but firmly.

"My apologies for the slip of tongue, Your Majesty," I said. "But I had thought Changelings could only... well, is that not normal?"

"An aberration. Changelings take a single form, but this one altered," one of the courtiers said, his hair the violent purple one only saw on Teletubbies and bad '80s cartoons. "A mutation caused by the pollutants in your world."

"Iron?" I guessed.

"If only that were the only poison in your world." The courtier sniffed and opened his mouth, his hand rising, body leaning forward as he worked up to an epic rant. Only to be shut down by a single walnut tossed at his head by Rhiannon.

"Hush. My aunt has no desire to hear you rant. Nor I."

"My apologies, my queen." The courtier bowed low.

Dismissing him, Rhiannon looked at me. "So. What do you seek from us?"

"Knowledge, if you will." I mentally ran through what I needed. "Knowledge of who hired the Changeling would be gratefully accepted. If you have it. If not... I would not dare ask for more."

"Polite, aren't you?" Rhiannon's eyes crinkled in amusement. "Not like your last... three masters?"

"I believe you're thinking of others. My second-last master was quite respectful. But I don't think you met him," Lily said softly.

"Oh, of course. I forget. You've had so many."

My eyes narrowed at the barbed words, and I glared at the woman. Queen. Fae. Whatever. Bitch was better. But I kept my tongue in my mouth because Lily had warned me not to anger her, even as much as declining her invitation. Which Lily hadn't said for the Mage Council.

"I know nothing of this Changeling's activities. As I said, we have little to do with your world anymore. At least, not officially," Rhiannon said. "Only a few things interest us these days."

I stilled, wondering what she meant. But seeing that she had no information for me, I bowed again. "Thank you for your time then, Your Majesty."

Rather than dismiss me, Rhiannon fixed Lily with a playful, indulgent smile. Like a cat staring at a struggling mouse. "Tell me, Aunt, have you told him who you are really?" At Lily's silence, she turned to me. "Have you asked her?"

I shook my head before realizing I didn't need to answer the damn woman.

When I opened my mouth to say that, she cut me off. "Of course not. Her masters are always in such a rush to use her powers, for their wishes, that they never ask what the price of those wishes are. Well, almost all of them."

"I know the price, but Lily's…"

Free? Even I could not say that word with a straight face. She had freedom, more than she'd had for many years, centuries, maybe ever since she was trapped in the ring. But she was not free. *Content?* Maybe. Though perhaps distracted was a better word. Distracted by games, my TV, by virtual reality and a million other things that kept her from thinking of, well, freedom.

For the first time, I considered how Lily might feel. Knowing that my death would send her to an abyss. Forever.

But even as I considered those words, Rhiannon spoke. "My aunt is not who you think she is. She was trapped not because she was too powerful, but for what she did. What she is." Rhiannon leaned forward. "You see her as a friend. A confidant. Do not be fooled."

"Rhiannon." Lily's voice was cold, angry.

The threat was clear, but Rhiannon ignored her. Ignored her because Lily was, in the end, powerless to do anything.

"You are quiet." Rhiannon's lips curled up, her eyes gleaming with amusement. "Good. You are listening. Then hear this, Mage. The one whose magic you use, whose knowledge you borrow? She is Lilith. Eldest of our kind. Mistress of magic, mother of monsters, the first rebel."

"Oh, please!" Lily rolled her eyes. "Not those lies again."

"Lies?" Rhiannon's lips curled. "You are the one who formalized, who began the rituals of magic. Whose experiments created the first jinn from the very blood that flows through your veins. You destroyed towns and wiped out settlements because they angered you."

"They tried to kill me!" Lily snapped.

"And they all deserved it?"

"Well…" Lily fell silent, shaking her head. "It was a long time ago. I was—"

"Powerful. A rival for the dragons themselves. And since then, you have grown only more powerful," Rhiannon said, looking at my hand where the ring rested. "Trapped, perhaps, but each year, each decade, you grow in strength and knowledge. Refining your magic."

"Now I'm being condemned for studying the only thing I can?" Lily said, clenching her fists. "Henry, I'm not—"

"You are. Lilith. And you're friends with creatures from legends and have a goddess who calls you auntie," I said, offering the jinn a half-smile. "I'm not dumb. I figured that one out a while ago." As Lily's jaw dropped, I turned back to Rhiannon and offered her a bow. "Thank you for your warning, Your Majesty. If that is all?"

Rhiannon's lips tightened. The mouthy courtier stirred, looking at me predatorily but made no move. We stood there in silence as I waited for Rhiannon to dismiss me. Or attack me. Either or.

In the end, the bounds of tradition, of the fae's word and their rules of hospitality, held. Rhiannon flicked her hand, sending me off, and I hurried away, only wiping my brow when I was out of sight. Perhaps she had considered killing me. Perhaps she had just intended to warn me. But I decided there and then never to return to Faery. Not without a lot more firepower anyway.

Beside me, a silent jinn walked. Until we stepped across the threshold and the ring's bindings forced her to disappear once more. Leaving me in peace, but with doubts. For while I knew who she had been, the question of her fate rose once more.

As much as I liked Lily, there was a reason why she had been locked up. A reason why so many feared her. And a reason, in the end, for me to keep the ring to myself. Because at least I knew what I would do with it.

Chapter 10

There was blessed solitude when I walked to the light rail train twenty minutes away. The entire journey would take just over two hours, more than enough time to think. More than enough time to…

That was where my thoughts stuttered to a stop. Truth was, I was not sure what I was supposed to think. I had known who Lily was for a long time. Suspected that her imprisonment were for crimes. Even if Lily wasn't exactly the Lilith from the Bible, it was likely much of her story was taken as inspiration. The same way the great flood might not mean the flooding of the world but a specific location. Of course, knowing that there are angels and faith magic had… well, let's say that I am agnostic.

None of which was an answer to my problem—if it was a problem—or solved my concerns about Lily. Or the ring. Even if she was properly punished—and a couple thousand years of imprisonment and forced servitude seemed a tad harsh—I was not entirely sure there was any way for me to free her. A glance at the ring made me wince as I recalled the only time I'd ever looked at the ring properly. The most complex enchantment I'd ever done had been the wards on our house. It'd taken over three months, spaced between classes and jobs and was, in my view, as good as, if not better than, the enchantments on my staff. There were multiple levels to the house enchantment, from increasing the durability of the walls to blocking scrying, alerting me of scrying attempts that couldn't be blocked, attack wards, and more.

Now, if one took the complexity of that ward, multiplied it by a thousand, stuffed it into the space of a single ring, you would get a glimpse of how complex the enchantment was. The fact that the ring was drawing power from an unknown source was even more frightening, since disrupting the enchantments themselves could have explosive consequences. Literally.

I swiped my card at the rail station and headed up the stairs. I was fortunate enough to get an empty car that pulled away moments after I got onboard. I found a side seat and pulled out my warding tablet to adjust and empower it. The modified Force Bubble sprung into existence, anchored around the ward and offering me some peace of mind.

"Damn fey," I muttered, looking about the empty rail car.

I was seated parallel to the walls and the doors, the few horizontally aligned seats empty but unappetizing in their restriction. Perhaps it was the look in that fey's eyes or perhaps it was the memory of being targeted, but I felt the need for space. For… freedom.

But that's not something Lily would ever have. Not while I held the ring. Not while anyone held the ring. And yet, who was I to judge? While I was not entirely oblivious, I knew I was not the best at reading people. Someone, sometime, decided this was a just punishment. Someone—or someones—more powerful, more skilled than me.

Yet could any punishment that read "for all eternity" ever be just? What kind of action, what sin could justify a punishment that lasted forever? And if no crime could justify eternity, then had Lily suffered enough?

Was what she was going through punishment or containment? Was she trapped because she did something wrong or because we—they—feared her? Feared what she could do? We didn't let nukes walk around unwatched. Why would people—jinn—be any different? Yet trapping her, punishing her…

Was it punishment for the crime or do we hope of redemption? In the belief that people would, could, change? Perhaps that was the question. Perhaps that was the answer, if it was a punishment. If we saw her enslavement as a punishment, then the question was is it just? But if we saw it as a way for her to redeem herself—eventually—then the question was, did I think she had changed? Do I think people could change?

My mind spun around in circles and whorls, forced to contort around my inconclusive thoughts. I couldn't figure out an answer. Maybe because there was no right answer. It's not a math problem where one plus one equaled two. It was a human problem, where one plus one might equal happily ever after or a gunshot to the foot.

I was so caught up in my thoughts that I hadn't noticed the train pull to a stop or the new passengers. Didn't see them even as the doors closed and trapped me with them. Didn't notice the gun that came up and fired as the train pulled away from the station.

The bullet punched through the air, hitting the Force Bubble. The idea for the ward was stolen directly from a scifi series. Anything moving slowly—a clap on the shoulder, a gesture from my hands—only slowed and angled away slightly. But the higher the momentum of the motion, the faster something moved, the greater the force my ward applied to it. It was a useful ward to use while I was in public, since it was only mildly disconcerting for mundanes caught in its vicinity. Unfortunately, I'd yet to work out a stable formula for movement, so it was only useable when the ward center was still.

The bullet hit the edge of the Force Bubble and slowed perceptibly. A lateral force was applied to the bullet, shifting it away from the center of the ward and making it fly by my face, leaving a sting of wind behind. They were smart enough to shoot for my head—avoiding my enchanted jacket—but that made the target much smaller. Even a small force was enough to make the shot miss, though the retort from the gun was still painful to my ears, even when slowed and distorted by my now-glowing modular ward tablet.

Instinct took over as I formed a Force Wall before me. Fingers snapped and twisted as I blocked off the area just outside of my Force Bubble. As the wall formed, it struck aside the gun barrel, sending the next shot up into the roof of the train. A mental command turned off the strained ward, the tablet glowing with light as it ran out of the Mana I instilled in it. Through my semi-opaque Force Wall, I stared at my attackers.

Three individuals. Clad in black business suits and shades at night, all of which spelled trouble. Of course, the trio of silencer-equipped pistols pointed at me was another good indicator. They were a mix of races—Hispanic and Caucasian—and ages, with the youngest a teenager. The kid's gun came back down to point at me and the shield I had formed, targeted straight at my face. Then they opened fire and my Force Wall flickered, points of impact spreading and rippling even as bullets ricocheted away.

Gunman 1 (Level 37)
HP: 100/100
MP: 0/0

Gunman 2 (Level 45)
HP: 100/100
MP: 0/0

Gunman 3 (Level 59)
HP: 100/100
MP: 0/0

Non-magical gunmen. Mortal, but dangerous nonetheless as assessed by Lily. That probably meant training—special forces or worse. After all, a normal cop on the beat was only in the low 20s and that's because he had a gun in hand and some modicum of training.

As the trio realized they were not getting through my Force Wall—not with their bullets ricocheting around—they stopped firing. They took turns dropping their magazines and reloading while keeping their guns pointed at me, faces impassive. A shard of a broken bullet seemed to have caught Gunman Two across the cheek, as a thin line of blood dripped down his face, ignored.

"Who are you people?" I said, keeping my spell formed as I mentally prepare a second and third backup.

Those bullets were unenchanted. They also had quite a bit of kick—especially compared to the pop-guns most gangers use—but nothing my Force Wall couldn't handle. Their only chance was lost when they missed me the first time. So I could afford to fish for information.

Rather than answer me, the lead gunner looked sideways, ignoring the screams and shouts of horror from passengers in other cabins. I followed the gunner's glance and spotted the upcoming stop, the way they eyed the doors.

"Come on. Just tell me. Who wants me dead?" I said.

Again, I got no answer. I noticed the pair at the back angling their bodies as they dropped their off-hands, taking them out of my view. Then the train slowed down, wheels grinding and shrieking, drowning out shrieking voices as it swayed ever so slightly.

"You failed. So tell me who sent you."

No one answered. But the doors hissed open and the passengers in the other cars rushed out. So did my attackers, though not before they tossed a pair of small oblong objects at my wall. I didn't have time to register what they were as I released my spell. The gunmen got their feet in the doorway and slammed headfirst into the Force Walls I'd formed around the car, hemming them in.

Force Cube Cast
Synchronicity: 89%
Durability: 1238

Foreheads smashed, bodies piled up against the wall and bounced backward. Their eyes widened, the youngest glancing back at the discarded items. I followed his gaze, spotted the grenades, and winced. Before everything became chaos.

***

In the resulting bedlam of two grenades exploding in a contained space, I sneaked out of the train via the untouched back doors. I couldn't hear anything but the incessant ringing in my ears, bag slung over my shoulder as I cast a simple Glamour that changed what I looked like. I combined that with an Illusion for the security cameras, though I was not entirely sure how useful that'd be with the cameras in the rail car having already caught a glimpse of me.

Then again, I was sure my other guardians would cover it up. If they weren't the ones who'd sent my attackers. Because… well, I was not entirely sure who else had three trained, mundane killers with access to high explosives and silenced weapons. Then again, with the militarization of our society, that number was rather higher and more depressing than I liked considering.

Behind me, as I hurried away on foot, I left the burnt and wrecked shells of my enemies, corpses torn and twisted by the rebounding explosive force of the grenades. I'd created the cube to contain them, to potentially get some answers. I hadn't expected a grenade, and even now, I could feel how low my Mana was, how drained I'd been reinforcing the spell as the explosion rebounded. Even if I had grown more powerful, even if the Force Cube was one of my more complex spells—which I would never have tried casting if they hadn't given me the time to do so—it was still tiring to use.

As I hurried out of the chaotic station, I couldn't help but feel a little guilty at the deaths I'd caused, the collateral damage that was done. I hated killing, and even if I hadn't done it myself, their deaths were painful. Still, if there was one thing I'd learned, it was that at least two groups were after me. Because whoever had sent the doppelganger wasn't likely to use something this mundane.

Letting out an exhalation, I ducked into a nearby alleyway and recast both spells, cloaking myself in magic. It was time to get home. Quietly.

***

"You're not allowed out without me," Alexa stated. There was no anger in her voice, though she stared at me till I offered her a nod. Once I got back—later than the night-shift-working ex-Initiate—I'd been grilled in detail about my encounter.

"The police offering any more news?" I asked, tilting my head toward the TV that wasn't on a superhero TV show or console game, but the local news for once. Even if I'd contained the blast, the damage done to the train and the ensuing disruption was more than enough for the local news to jump on it.

"No," Alexa said.

Unasked and unanswered was the question of whether I should be packing an extra bag for a long, long talk with the police. And maybe jail time.

I hoped not. While I did have a bucket list, jail wasn't on it.

Leaving might be an option, but that meant abandoning our house and the wards. Even if I did leave, it'd be a temporary solution. Sooner or later, my enemies would find me.

"So…" I let my voice draw out, looking at Alexa and the silent Lily.

"I'll…" Alexa frowned then shrugged. "I'll ask around. See if I can learn if you're in trouble. If we can learn who it is."

Lily offered me a half-smile, then flashed the old Quest again. The one that asked me to stay alive. I couldn't help but snort, wishing this was a game. One that railroaded you with clues, rather than a stupid puzzle one where the solution might be right in front of you—or in a portion of the map that you'd missed half the game back.

"I guess I'll just rest for now," I said, feeling the lack of Mana sending another wave of exhaustion through me. Being low on Mana and paranoid had drained me, putting me on the edge of sleep.

The pair offered me a smile, waving me away as I stumbled up the stairs. I barely even glanced at the notification that told me of a Level increase, knowing it didn't help.

Perhaps, perhaps a solution would present itself when I awakened.

Chapter 11

Two days passed in tense silence, Alexa's few contacts unable to offer us any assurance. Even our attempts to speak to our governmental guardians were thwarted—the ever-present service vans that had been parked on our street for months gone.

We'd been left in the dark, so I spent my time working on the enchantments. I finished the portable shelter, then worked the portable flamethrowers while we waited for the next shoe to drop. Alexa had taken a leave of absence from her job, though they'd hinted that she might not be welcome back. Actions had consequences, and mine had lost her her job.

When a knock came on the door, I didn't move from my work table, having nearly completed the weapons. After I was done, I planned to work on my staff. The layered defenses available on the staff would be greatly appreciated, even if—unlike the flamethrowers—I'd have to power the staff myself.

When Alexa lead Caleb into the room, I looked up, blinking in surprise at the Mage. "You're back."

"I am. I come bearing conflicted news," Caleb said. "The Council is unwilling to risk further manpower on an untested warlock."

"Mage," I said, glaring at Caleb. I might not have been trained by the Mage Council, but I was a Mage. Bette than their apprentices.

"Warlock in their eyes. Many do not believe what I have reported, are unwilling to accept your potential," Caleb said. "It is why I have bargained for you to take the apprentice examination early."

"What?" I said.

"Pack your staff. We must leave if we are to make it to the examination." Caleb gestured to the staff propped up beside me as my next project.

"I'm nearly done," I said, gesturing at the tubes.

"Those things?" Caleb took one glance and sniffed. "They're cumbersome and not worth the Mana invested. You should have spent your time on the staff."

"Funny. But I like having more tools." I looked Caleb over, shaking my head. "Not as if you don't have your own enchantments."

"They are accessories. Useful but unimportant compared to a proper staff," Caleb said. "That we are forced to leave them behind by modern-day fashion does not reduce the staff's functionality."

"Yeah, yeah, yeah. Heard it before."

"You are right. Now, come."

I dithered for a moment, not entirely sure I wanted to commit. But what choice did I have? At least the Mage Council was still willing to help. No matter how much I grew, no matter what Level I achieved, I'd still be outnumbered. As much as I might have disliked the Council, I needed them. I needed an organization at my back.

Letting out a breath, I grabbed my staff and stood.

Alexa cleared her throat, drawing my attention. "Didn't we agree to something?"

"Sorry. You're right. Is she allowed to come?" I looked at Caleb, who shook his head.

"Can you guarantee his safety?" Alexa asked, looking pointedly at Caleb.

"During the trial, yes." Caleb cocked his head. "I can take you to the grounds. Outside. If he fails—"

"We're on our own," Alexa said. "I'll get my spear."

I tossed her the pair of finished flamethrowers. "Add this too."

The blonde nodded, heading upstairs to get dressed and armed. Caleb sniffed, tapping his foot only to be brought up short when Lily stood.

"Leave us, Mage," Lily said.

"I'm—"

"Waiting outside."

Caleb narrowed his eyes, but when I cleared my throat, he relented and left, leaving Lily and me to stare at one another.

"We haven't… talked since, you know," Lily said awkwardly. "About me. About my… crimes."

"Were they crimes?" I said.

Lily nodded.

"Were they bad?"

Lily nodded again.

"Bad enough to be put in a ring for all eternity?"

"I… don't know."

I nodded. "Yeah, thought so. We don't have much to talk about then."

Lily flinched, looking at the tops of her feet.

I winced, realizing how harsh that sounded, and put a hand on her arm. "Lily." When she looked up, I offered her a small smile. "It's fine. Whatever you did, it was a long time ago. So long it's probably not relevant anymore." When Lily flinched, I raised an eyebrow. "Never mind. It's still not relevant. You're you now. Not… whatever."

"We're still friends, right?" Lily said, sounding timid.

"Don't have a choice, do I?" I said, trying for teasing.

When Lily shrank back, I winced and decided to shut up. I hugged the jinn, feeling the tension in her body that slowly relaxed and went away. Eventually Alexa cleared her throat, reminding me that I had to go.

"We're friends. Now and forever. Promise," I said. "But I got to go."

Lily nodded, pushing me away. I headed off, catching her words just before I left.

"Good luck."

***

Mundane. That's a good description of my magical existence. No magical carpets, no teleporting rings, just a black four-door sedan that takes me out of the city and down the highway. Alexa's seated in the back, dressed in her armored jacket and skirt, spear taken apart and laid out beside her. I'm up front with Caleb, watching as he guides us down the road with expert ease.

"No enchantments on the car?" I said, having finished looking it over.

"It's a rental."

As I said. Mundane.

"You should consider going over what you have learnt. There is no time to fix your staff," Caleb said. "But some last-minute cramming would not hurt."

"Actually, did you know that research has shown that last-minute cramming might actually be more detrimental than studying?" I flashed Caleb a smile, only to have him glare at me briefly before turning his gaze back to the road. "Fine. If I fail, you know who I'm going to blame." When the silence grew colder, I added, "Me."

"You're really not as funny as you think, Henry," Alexa said.

I grumbled under my breath but closed my eyes, calling forth what I knew about the examination. There were three sections in an apprentice exam. The first was theory—which mostly consisted of a written examination where I had to expound on formulas. This was my weakest area, and the area Caleb was hinting that I work on. While Lily might dump information into my mind, the way she did so was specific to spells, such that

---

I often found myself missing important areas of learning. Or at least I used to. Lessons with Caleb and more spells had helped patch those holes. If I had to describe it, it'd be like learning high school mathematics—algebra, differential equations, logarithmic charts—and then realizing that you'd never learned how to do long division. Or, say, angles in a circle. Gods, I hated those.

The second portion of the examination I was much more blasé about. That was the practical examination where you were asked to show your command over magic. Apprentices were scored on the effects of their spells, and since I was, in terms of actual casting, much more advanced, I expected to get close to full scores. Even spells that I might not "know," I could recreate by linking multiple aspects.

The last portion would be dealt with while I was writing the examination. That was where my staff would come into play, where I would provide the staff to them for review. They'd test the staff, reviewing it for flaws before marking it. I was much less certain of my results there. While I had some Master-level work in the staff, I was also still trying to make other portions of it work.

Still, I thought, overall, I should pass. But maybe a little more review of the theory would be best. Because passing wasn't my goal anymore. I needed to be so good that they wanted me in the Council, that they were willing to put in real effort.

Resolved to do more than just pass, I went over my spells and the theories in my mind, allowing time to pass.

***

Since I'd refused to go to the Mage Council's headquarters, the examination was being held in one of their many safe houses. In this case, it was a working horse farm. Stable? In either case, the farm had about four fenced off areas for the horses, a big stable, and another, larger covered riding ring on the right of the road. Dominating the entire location was the double-story white ranch house with its large windows and blue curtains. A trio of vehicles were parked outside, the truck being the only practical farm instrument. The other two were sedans like ours, city vehicles by the lack of dents and dirt.

Of course, my attention was drawn to the presence of the three examiners standing on the house-spanning front porch. How did I know they were my examiners and not stable hands? Well, their Levels for one.

Patricia Fitzgerald (Level 173)
HP: 180/180
MP: 1783/1894

Nicholas Diaz (Level 183)
HP: 141/147
MP: 1084/1147

Muhammad Black (Level 171)
HP: 201/204
MP: 997/1473

"Are all examiners that high level?" I muttered to Caleb as we got out of the car. I could feel the power radiating out from them, and Patricia had a half-dozen more enchantments on her than Caleb did. Obviously she didn't agree with his "the staff is the best thing ever" line of thought. I thought I might even like her.

"No. Your case is unique. They are the head examiners for the three closest regions," Caleb said.

Caleb stayed silent until we were close to the group, then he introduced us and them to one another. Of course, I didn't mention that I knew their names already thanks to Lily. Be a little rude.

"The Templar must stay outside." Muhammad stated that with a glare at Alexa.

"Ex-Templar," she said.

"There is no such thing," Muhammad snapped before running a hand across curly, close-cropped hair, glancing at my hand with Lily's ring. "The jinn is not here?"

"She stayed behind." Caleb added, after glancing at the ring, "In a manner of speaking."

"Good. The staff?" Nicholas held out his hand before inclining his head toward Patricia.

"Mage Fitzgerald will guide you to the examination room."

I stepped forward and handed over my staff, giving it one last glance before following Patricia into the house. She strode past the living room into the single barren office right off the corridor. On the worn, bulky office table, a paper had been set, along with a single line exercise book.

"Two hours."

I acknowledged her words and walked over, fishing some pens from inside my jacket before putting the jacket over the back of the chair and getting comfortable. Patricia looked me over once again then walked out, shutting the door. I felt the spell that sealed the room and triggered the protective enchantment. For a moment, fear clutched at me—until I noticed the trigger that would turn the room-sealing enchantment off from the inside. Right. Not a prison, just extra careful against cheaters who might be getting help from others.

I snorted, tapped the workbook, and flipped over the examination questions. Best to get to it then. I scanned through the first question and clicked my pen, composing my thoughts. Time to get to it.

Two hours went by in a blink. I wrote and wrote, answering questions as quickly as I could. At first, the questions were easy to answer. The equivalent of basic math. But by the time I got toward the last couple of pages, the complexity made me frown, my brow furrowing as I struggled to provide responses. Some of it was history, context dependent. Others required knowledge of spell formulae and theorems I only vaguely recalled, or had puzzled out the basic portions of. I was so caught up in answering, I didn't notice the door opening, the release of the wards.

"Time is up." Patricia stood beside the table, hand held out for me to hand her the notebook.

I blinked, staring at the words I'd scribbled, and saw a notification that had my eyes narrowing in thought.

Experience Gained for Theorem Exploration!
+27,489

"Oh, you tricky bastards," I said, looking at Patricia's impatient mien and the last few pages. I scooted back slightly as I reached forward with both hands, gripped the last few questions, and ripped out the pages. I saw Patricia hiss, and as I set the pages on fire, I barely felt the trace of power as she extinguished the flames. I felt another wave of power, and I stopped trying to destroy the paper. "You just copied my answers, didn't you?"

Patricia sniffed. "We will not be marking the torn portions."

"Bullshit." I tossed the notebook on the table, ignoring her still-extended hand, and stood. Sons of bitches caught me out, making me think I was taking an apprentice exam but instead testing me for what I really knew. Testing me for the things that Lily had taught me behind their backs.

I stalked out of the house, only to see Caleb waiting for me. His lips pursed at my glare, but I wasn't about to be mollified. "That was no apprentice test."

"The initial part was," Caleb said, holding up his hands. "I did not know they were going to test you like that. But it's good, it means they're taking you seriously."

"Or trying to trick Lily's knowledge out of me."

"Knowledge that you would have to share anyway, if you joined us," Patricia said, appearing from behind me. "I have marked your examination."

"Already?" I said, surprised.

"Yes. Your basics are spotty, but much better than most of our Apprentices, I will admit. You also have, as Magus Hahn has informed us, quite a degree of knowledge in some advance application of spell theory."

I narrowed my eyes, hearing the but. "But?"

"Theory is insufficient to prove your ability. And it seems your work with the staff is, at best, average," Patricia said.

Once again I narrowed my eyes in suspicion at the Mage. I was not entirely sure I agreed with her assessment, knowing what I did of the Mage Council. Alexa, seated on the hood of the car, looked at me and I carefully shook my head to keep her seated. No, nothing that she could help with here.

"So what? We finishing this?" I said, deciding to see what else they wanted. Or needed.

"This way," Patricia said, stepping past me and heading for the indoor riding circle.

I followed, the giant white canvas flaps billowing in the wind as I walked into the bare earth riding circle. The riding circle was empty but for a series of enchanted staves located at the borders of the stable. As I stepped in, I felt the enchantments kick in, sealing me within.

A hand came up, generating a shield across my body even as I put distance between Patricia and myself. I continued my scan of the location, noting the presence of the other examiners and my staff, held casually in one tester's hand. A jerk of my fist triggered the return protocols in my staff, making it lurch through the air to slap into my hand.

"Calm yourself," Caleb said, holding up a hand. "The enchantments are to ensure that no damage is done to the surroundings."

I looked at the Mage and saw that he and Patricia were not making any threatening moves. Neither were the other examiners, truth be told. And... well, that made sense. I found myself flushing in embarrassment even as I pushed down the emotion. After all, they could have warned me. Unlike most of their apprentices, I dealt with more violent and dangerous situations regularly.

"Now what?"

"Now you show us you can handle yourself," Nicholas said, waving toward the center of the room.

A second later, a giant ball of glowing light, made from criss-crossing verses of spell formula, appeared. My eyes narrowed. I was surprised he'd managed to conjure something so complex with a wave of his hand—until I noticed the small tripod and globe beneath the actual globe itself. Ah. An enchanted object.

"You want me to read the spell formulas?" I guessed, cocking my head as I tried to follow the scrolling information.

Tough, especially since I could only see portions of the spell. Though even a quick glance told me that multiple spells were involved in the creation of the globe. In fact, some of those spells looked familiar—like that Fire Bolt one...

A fraction of a second later, a Fire Bolt formed in the center of the spell globe and shot toward me. I batted it aside with my shield, frowning. The spell was quite weak, so weak that it probably wouldn't have killed me. Probably.

"What the hell?" I said. That was not how the examination was supposed to go.

"You will need to read, anticipate, and understand the spells formed by the globe and counter them. The testing globe will continue to release spells at timed intervals. Points will be awarded for spells that are blocked or counter-spelled," Nathan said. As he finished, next to the spell globe, a scoreboard appeared with the number 001 on it. "You will need to score a minimum of a hundred to pass."

When I opened my mouth to ask further questions, an Ice Bolt formed around the globe and shot toward me. Once again, I batted it away, watching as the points went up by another one.

"A word of warning. As time goes on, the spells you will have to deal with grow more complicated," Mohammad said, offering me a thin smile.

I growled softly, keeping my shield up while focusing on the spell globe again. The new spell formula running across the globe was one that was familiar to me, and so while the spell globe formed the spell, I reached out with my Mana and disrupted the spell.

Mana Bolt Counter Spell Cast
Synchronicity: 89%

I received three points as the Mana Bolt fizzled out, its spell container disrupted by my injection of Mana. Counter-spelling came in many forms, but the one I had been taught was simple—the use of my Mana injected into the forming spell container, splicing my spell formula amendment to it. Of course, counter-spelling was complicated. You couldn't throw random "numbers" at another spell formula, hoping they would stick. You had to actually know which portion you were targeting with your splice. On top of that, each spell had gaps within their formula, areas where you could slide in your own Mana and spell formula. Miss those areas, and even if you knew what you wanted to adjust, you would still fail.

Counter-spelling basically required you to understand the spell formula being used and also be extremely quick at casting, since you were, in many ways, casting both the spell itself and the spell injector.

At first, I racked up points fast, counter-spelling everything the globe threw at me. The initial stages were simple—spells like Gust, Burn, Light, and the like were used in a combative form. Buckets of acid, sparks of electricity, and even waves of conjured water scrolled through the globe and were disrupted. I had to give it to the Mage Council—the spell globe was actually a good training tool. The wide variety of spell containers, delays in spell formation, and alteration in Mana channeling all required me to be inventive in my counters. But good tool or not, if this was the level of difficulty, this would be a cakewalk.

Ten minutes later, I was feeling the strain. My total score crossed the sixty-point range and my Mana dropped below half. From a slow and steady stroll, the spell formula had sped up, rolling past faster than the noob zone chat window on launch day. I'd stopped being able to read the spell itself and instead resorted to guessing. Which had obvious results.

"Head's up!" I twisted at the hips and slammed the decahedron of platinum into the air with my staff.

The force applied to the end of my staff was enough to numb both hands and nearly tear the staff out of my hands entirely. Thankfully, it was still considered a win. My count went up by another point and the spell globe burped, another spell forming.

"Foolish," Nicholas muttered to Muhammad.

Sadly, I couldn't disagree. I stopped trying to counter-spell, my latest attempt a definite failure, and instead focused on defense. That meant I'd have to deal with a lot more spells, but better that than failure. To begin, I reconstructed my Force Shield, shrinking its size so that it only covered my body. Next, I curved the wall so that I wasn't taking attacks straight-on. Not a moment too soon either, as the spell finished and a series of spinning air daggers flew toward me.

An academic portion of my mind noted that the air daggers weren't contained once they were released, but instead they used a series of three points to make themselves. First, the point of origin, the second about halfway toward me, and the third very close to where I stood. The last two target points adjusted the air pressure and direction of airflow, guiding the air daggers that had been formed at the first target point.

The shield took the individual attacks with aplomb, the air daggers bouncing off with the sound of a bad dubstep, making me smirk. But already the next spell was forming and I was reading its data.

Holding the Force Shield was easy, but considering I had another forty spells to go, I considered better, more interesting options. Because each moment I held the Shield, my Mana dropped. As I grasped the content of the next spell, I dismissed the Shield and jumped straight into the air, using a quick cast of Gust to elevate me even higher. A second later, the ground burst into verdant greenery, grasping vines searching for me. I let loose a second burst of the spell, keeping me in the air while flattening the already dying vines.

And not once did I shift my gaze from the spell globe as another spell scrolled past. Only to be joined by a second scrolling formula.

"Two!" I growled.

But I raised my staff, invoking the pre-made shield in the spell to deal with the first spell formula. All the while trying to grasp what the second spell formula was. It seemed they were intent on ramping up the difficulty.

***

Five spells. None of them were particularly complex—Force Spears, Mana Bolt, Freezing Rain, and the like—but each of them was enough to knock me out. Five spells scrolled past at a clip, forming from the globe and targeted at me.

All around me, the ground had been torn up, baked, and frozen. If not for the spelled enchantments around the perimeter, the entire riding stable would have been destroyed already. The acrid scent of materials materialized then dismissed lingered, traces of acid, ozone, and burnt soil assaulting my senses. Each breath I took made my chest heave, my Mana levels barely above "Henry is conscious" levels.

Five spells. I began triple casting again, the first the counter-spell container, then splitting the container to hold the counter-spells for each of the injections I was using to break two of the five spells. In my hand, my staff glowed, helping to draw Mana into my spells, while the Force Shield blocked off the remainder attacks.

As the strain of managing multiple spells increased my headache, I gestured with my hand, snapping it forward. A flicker of information showed the low Synchronicity rates—barely in their forties—but I ignored them, even as the lack of proper casting drained more Mana. Rather, I focused on the three spells that were aimed at me.

Frost Spear, Wind Drill, and Metal Missiles all slammed into my Force Shield. I angled the shield to take the Spear on the corner, allowing it to glance off sideways and strike the enchanted protections behind. The Missiles were like raindrops striking my shield, plentiful and annoying but not dangerous in and of themselves. The Wind Drill curved at the last second, taking my shield straight-on. I growled, trying to reinforce the spell only for the increased force in the spinning Drill to shatter it. I threw myself backward, attempting to dodge the attack, but I could only watch as the Wind Drill neared my chest, ready to punch through.

Just before it could strike, Mohammad waved and the Drill dispersed, sending a blast of air that ruffled my hair even as I landed on the ground. A sharp pain radiated from my tailbone and I groaned, making a mental note to look into enchanted underwear again. As I struggled to my feet with the aid of my staff, I surreptitiously rubbed my bottom while glancing at the scoreboard. For the first time in a while, I had time to really look at it.

117.

"Har. Beat it." I sniggered and slowly limped over to the testers.

Five spells might be my limit, it seemed. I absently eyed the experience notifications I'd received. The spell globe really was a great training tool, one that had pushed my comprehension and analysis of spells to a level I'd never had to get to.

"So do I get a nifty top hat or something?" I flashed the trio of examiners and Caleb a smile, only to find them staring at me in silence.

Chapter 12

"So what do apprentices get?" I repeated, waiting for the trio to speak.

The Mage Council examiners regarded me as if I were a bug that had crawled out of a movie theater seat, replete with stale popcorn and spilled soda. It was not the gaze of congratulations, which was rather interesting considering I should have passed.

"You were right," Mohammad said to Caleb.

"I told you." Caleb hocked a thumb toward me. "Though it seems that Mage Tsien has been holding back on me a little."

"By… thirty points, I would say." Nicholas sniffed. "It does not bode well for us trusting the warlock."

"Mage," I grumbled while rubbing my bum. I kept my head down though, since the one thing I really didn't want them to grasp was how I'd soft-balled the entire test. I could have continued counter-spelling longer than I did, and I definitely could have continued to deal with the spells. While my Mana shortage was real—hard to hide that fact—how fast I was losing it and how fast I could regenerate it was something I was trying to hide still. After being tricked once, I wasn't going to be dumb enough to reveal all my cards.

"Not if we don't say so," Nicholas said, glaring at me. He looked at my staff for a second, considering the piece of wood in my hand, before he turned to the others. "Your judgment?"

Patricia glanced at the spell globe then at me once more and nodded. "He has passed every test we have set. He is at the apprentice level at the least. A full Mage of the sixth circle."

I blinked, knowing there were seven circles, with those in the inner circles—the lower numbers—the most powerful. Caleb was considered part of the second circle these days. In that sense, I'd skipped the entire Apprentice level—or seventh circle—to become a journeyman. But it'd be at least one more circle before I could be considered a full member. In their view.

"Perhaps, but we are judging more than his academic ability," Nicholas said. "He lacks discipline and the right mindset. His work is sloppy, if prone to brilliance. Though, I would venture, much of the latter is due to his jinn. Otherwise, he is middling at best."

I narrowed my eyes but turned to Mohammad, who had started speaking. "Brilliance that we could harness. The theories he expounded upon in his essay are interesting. Both Beckett's Theorem of Fundamental Formulas and Obibje Principle of Sevens were quite illuminating. I do not believe the combination Mr. Tsien recommended would work as well as he thought, but perhaps if we combined the Ozmas Principle—"

"Enough. No one wants to hear you prattle. Are you for or against his inclusion in our ranks?" Nicholas snapped.

"Well, he has passed our tests. I think, in that sense, we should at the least let him know our conditions," Mohammad said.

Patricia nodded firmly, making me frown as Caleb stepped forward to speak.

"What conditions?" I said suspiciously.

"I told you the Council would have requirements of you. If we are to acknowledge you as one of us, if we are protect you, certain matters must be agreed on." Caleb took a breath and forged on. "You'll need to swear a binding oath to be loyal to the Council. And that, on your death, you would hand over the ring."

"And no more hiding of your secrets." Nicholas crossed his arms. "You will share everything that your jinn teaches you."

"A binding oath?" My eyes narrowed. "I'm assuming you're talking a blood oath?"

"No. A soul oath," Caleb said.

I hissed, and even Patricia looked uncomfortable. I wasn't surprised she was uncomfortable considering what a soul oath actually consisted of. Like its name, it bound me by my soul—the center of my being—rather than my body. Those oaths were nearly impossible to break, and when they were broken, they left the oathbreaker a shattered creature. Monsters were created when soul oaths broken, because the mind didn't break—just the things that made us human.

"You can't seriously think I'll agree to that," I said.

"If you desire our help, you will." Nicholas said, stopping Caleb when he tried to say something else. "You have little choice here."

"Pretty sure no is still valid."

Nicholas snorted, his gaze flicking to my ring then my face. "You could not even stand five spells. If I wanted to take that ring—"

"You'd fail." I shook my head and turned, walking to the car. I paused when a thought struck, my eyes narrowing as I turned around. "You are going to drive me back, right?"

"Henry, you need to consider your position more carefully," Caleb said, concern in his voice. "This might not be what you want. What I wanted. But the Council has made it clear that they want more from you."

My fist clenched as I looked at the all-too-smug Nicholas and the prideful Mohammad before turning to the conflicted Patricia. They thought they had me in a corner. That I had no choice but to accede to their demands. And truth be told, they were right. Lily's protection might stop over-Leveled assholes like these guys from attacking me, but it did nothing to stop them from sending waves of appropriately Leveled assholes. And unlike a game, I wouldn't gain much experience from protecting myself from them, because my Levels were tied to my ability to both physically manage and understand the magic that was input in my body.

Angry or not, I was in a corner. They were right. But… "I already did. I'm not taking a soul oath. No way, no how."

"Then they'll kill you," Caleb said.

"So be it," I said. "No one's immortal, eh?"

"Bold words. But know that if you walk away now, when we speak again, your deal will be even worse," Nicholas almost snarled.

"Don't worry. I won't be."

"Foolish child…"

I didn't bother answering and walked out, deciding to stop being childish and arguing. I stalked forward until I reached the edge of the enchantment, which had yet to turn off. For a moment, I waited to see if they'd turn it off, and when they didn't, I pushed my staff against the enchantment. My eyes narrowed as the enchantments on the staff flared to life, pulling at the shielding wall. Information about the enchantment flowed into my mind via the analyzing runes in the staff. My eyes narrowed as I searched for the gaps, then when the next pulse from the shield cycled through, I inserted an adjustment.

A moment later, the enchantment opened up, splitting aside for me to walk out. Behind me, I heard a few indrawn breaths, but I refused to look back. If they'd been willing to bargain, to help out, perhaps we could have come up with something. Instead, they'd decided to hold my feet over the fire and see how much I'd squirm. Well, bugger that.

Alexa looked up when I came over, her eyes narrowing when she took in my distressed demeanor. She spun her spear around, watching the riding stable. There was no need to say anything, not with how things had gone.

When five minutes came and went and Caleb didn't come out, I groaned softly and fished out my phone.

"Looks like we're taking a carshare back," I said, glancing at Alexa's spear. "They won't attack us. Can't."

"Fine," Alexa said, opening the sedan's back door and fishing out her duffel. She looked at me and flashed a grin. "Shotgun."

"Hey! You can't do that until the car's here," I said, having finished booking our ride back.

"Nope. Called it."

"That's—aargh!" I threw up my hands and waved down the driveway. "Let's go wait on the main road."

Together, we walked out. I couldn't say for sure what Alexa was thinking, but for myself, I was debating how on earth we were going to survive.

***

"To sum up—the government has pulled back a couple of blocks. The Druids and the other pagans have left. So will the Mage Council. The Templars and the rest of the Orders are going to leave now that the Council has made their position known. And none of the other quieter guardians, those who want the ring, are going to stick around, not without the big boys in play," Lily said, ticking off on her fingers. We were back in the living room, after I'd explained what had happened with the Mage Council and my decision. "That sound about right?"

"Yeah. I doubt they're going to leave entirely, just in case I manage to level…" I turned my attention to Lily. "Can we do that?"

"Do what?" Lily said, raising an eyebrow.

"Can we raise my level? Hit 100, like, in a week or something and release me from the spell?" Even as I finished speaking, I realized how bad an idea that was. Exactly what did I intend to do even if I did get a higher level? It wasn't as if that higher level, artificially inflated or not, would do anything but release the wish.

"A bit. Not all the levels, but we could flood you with more experience," Lily said. "I'm not sure why…"

Alexa pointed at me. "We should get you to train. Properly."

"Properly?" I said, blinking.

Alexa nodded. "No more random silly quests, no more hunting for the best clothing or carving silly sticks. You train and level and increase how much Mana you can wield."

"Training montage?" I said with a slight smirk, only to get smacked on the arm by Alexa.

"Idiot. This isn't funny." Alexa said, shaking her head. "But we should also talk about leaving."

"Our lease isn't up," I objected immediately, thinking about my poor damage deposit. Our damage deposit. Huh. I wondered if the Templars would want their share back?

"We're talking about getting killed, Henry. Focus," Alexa snapped, and I sighed.

I pointed at the wards we had. "But the house is warded."

"You know those won't last forever. If they really wanted us dead, they could breach the wards," Alexa said. "Staying here, we're just a target. If they all leave..."

I nodded, looking at my hands. She's correct that there really isn't a better option than leaving. If we can run and hide—*if* being the operative word—we had a chance of lasting. Lasting long enough to... to what?

"Henry?" Lily said, cocking her head.

"How did your other owners manage to not get killed?" I said, frowning.

"Well, first, they generally hid my presence," Lily said. "And then, well, most didn't ask for magic. Money—when wished for properly—was easy enough to offer them. Power was harder, but it could be arranged. You have no idea how many political marriages I managed to arrange. But for the ones who wanted or needed magic, I was more of a research assistant, you know?

"Then, well, they became the most powerful Mage in their surroundings. And with the way news and rumors got distorted, no one was going to travel for weeks or months to check out a bad rumor. Or fight someone who could be more powerful than them just for the chance of getting an artifact that was better than the one they had already. Maybe."

I sighed, rubbing my face. "So you're saying air transportation and phone lines are killing me."

"Sort of? It's not as if a lot of my owners weren't killed because they had me," Lily said. "My last couple of owners before you never let anyone know of my presence. They hid my power and barely used me as more than a research assistant. So we're in new territory here."

"Yay," I said desultorily. "I always wanted to break new ground."

Alexa snorted, then poked me in the shoulder. "It doesn't matter. We just have to get you strong enough that you can fight them off."

"What? You mean the entire world?" I said.

"Or you could look for someone who's strong enough to do it already," Lily offered.

"Like?"

"Well… ummm… Mer's stuck. Hecate… well. You aren't the right sex. Abe's sleeping somewhere. The Eight won't talk to you. Umm…."

I didn't know who Lily was speaking about, but what she was saying was clear enough. None of the people Lily knew who could have protected us were going to. Which meant I would have to do it myself.

"Well, if we're going to go, we should figure out how. And where." Alexa flashed me a half-smile.

I sighed. "You have a plan, don't you?"

Before Alexa could say anything, we were rudely interrupted. The screech of a tire-burning turn was the only notice we received before a truck barreled toward us. My eyes widened as I stared at the incoming vehicle, watched as it struck the windows and living room's outer wall. Watched as my wards, never meant to handle a vehicle driving straight at us, flared to life and tried to keep the vehicle out.

And failed.

Chapter 13

The wards bled most of the momentum from the vehicle. Force Columns, generated initially as Force Spikes, reared from the floor, meant to block or injure those who came through the windows. It had been easier to enchant the entire wall with the same ward form rather than pick out just the walls. They hit the truck's undercarriage as they grew, throwing it upward and tearing up the shaft and other mechanical bits.

Rather than come all the way in and smash us into pieces, the truck stalled, two-thirds of its body in our residence, the last third held off the ground by the spike columns. I stared at the shattered front window and saw no one there. Gasoline tanks on the truck tumbled and creaked, dented and broken in the initial charge, but not exploding. Perhaps it was the other defensive portions of the ward or perhaps it was the Force Spikes, but whatever had been meant to set the gasoline on fire didn't go off. Yet I smelled the spilled gasoline, heard it dribbling to the ground as my ears recovered from the cacophony of sound that the truck had created when it slammed into our building.

"Shit. We're under attack!" I snarled, turning to Alexa. Only to see that my friend was only partially responsive, coming to her senses as a gash down one side of her head spilled blood. "Oh gods. Alexa!"

I looked at Lily only to see her untouched by dust cloud or injury, but staring in shock. Not at the truck, but the shattered monitor on her laptop.

Rather than waste time on her, I cast around for something, anything. And saw the rolled up enchanting circle, the portable habitat I'd been working on.

I snatched it from its place and threw it on the table before picking up Alexa with a heave and stepping into the circle. It hummed for a second as I shoved my Mana into the runes, powering them. As the walls of the habitat flickered to life, the gas tanks on the truck finally exploded. If not for the flash of magic I felt just before the tanks went off, I would have thought the explosion had something to do with the sparking electricity or the broken truck itself.

The world went red and orange, flames and pieces of the truck itself striking the Force Walls. But they held, having been reinforced for just such an occurrence. Well, this and more. Mana sucked out of my body, flooding down the runes, taking whatever I had recovered and a little more before the world flashed white again.

Just before we left, I caught a glimpse of Lily, untouched in the remnants of our home, looking forlorn and lost. Seated amidst flame and smoke as our home, our place of residence and relaxation, was destroyed.

And then we were gone.

***

Our forms blurred, transported through a parallel dimension, pulled apart and shifted before we were returned to harsh reality and the anchor point I had created, returned to the mark I'd set. I lurched forward, the motion that was not motion throwing off my sense of balance. I tumbled forward, holding onto Alexa, and only managed to twist enough to not drop her onto the ground.

As I pushed myself upward, Alexa weakly struggled out of my arms to fall onto her butt next to me. Pushing aside her hands, I shoved at the cut on her head, pushing it together while casting Heal. Thankfully, this spell was one I had grown so used to that I no longer needed to use a physical component to cast.

A few minutes later, Alexa pushed me aside and scrubbed at her face. She cleaned off the sticky blood that had congealed from the heat that had managed to touch us even through the barriers. While Alexa was busy cleaning herself off, I took stock of our surroundings. I touched a ward and sent my Mana into it, reinforcing the wards that had automatically gone up when we'd teleported in. Among other things, it was meant to hide our aura signatures and Lily's signature too. It wouldn't hold forever, but it would give me time to work on the next step.

Before I could get to that, Alexa spoke up. "Where are we?"

"Uh… well. Storage depot. About two miles from the house. I needed a place to test out teleportation wards, and I used to keep this for my, well, other business and forgot about it." I gestured at the variety of suitcases, storage chests, and random pieces of furniture I'd collected and never managed to sell. Or in some cases, kept because I felt I'd make more later.

Admittedly, after I got my magic, I'd forgotten about my rainy day stash. I'd only remembered the storage shack because I had been considering a place for my teleportation experiments. And, I'd admit, I'd spent a little more time building the wards around here due to a quest that Lily have given me.

Which reminded me that I needed to make sure Lily's signature and mine stayed hidden. That meant a moving enchantment ward. The easiest way to do that was to inscribe the enchanted ward on something easy to carry. Luckily, among the other things I kept here were small wooden blocks and scribing tools. In short order, I had a workplace set up.

"Alexa, can you find some string? I'm thinking necklaces," I asked before turning to the blocks.

It took a few minutes for me to recall the wards I'd considered but never created. Once more, I considered why I hadn't, why I had been willing to believe that my 'allies' would stick beside me. And cursed myself for the foolishness. Too late for regrets though. It was time to get to work, time to complete things I'd considered but not put into place.

Thirty minutes later, I had a pair of amulets. The first one suppressed and changed Alexa's aura—that had taken me less than five minutes to create. The second warded amulet took the rest of the time, what with my stronger aura and Lily's. I'd mentally planned a few ways of doing this. At first, I'd considered creating two wards—one for Lily's ring and one for myself. However, the math on that didn't work. Even the ambient aura from the ring meant that I would have to carry around a much larger, more powerful aura ward.

To fix the issue, I'd decided on something a little more creative. First, I subsumed the aura from the ring into mine. That made my aura much stronger while changing it. Once I had changed my aura, I needed to reduce its output. Of course, one of the aspects was that my aura was now so powerful, it was impossible to keep it suppressed on a daily basis. Instead, I altered it in stages by first compressing the ambient aura down to reduce the radius. I needed to do that multiple times until I stopped being a beacon. The result was that my compressed aura made me seem even more powerful than I was, but it required someone to be close to me to feel it.

At least, that was the theory. I gripped the amulet, slid it over my head, and drew a deep breath before activating the amulet. I felt a cold wind run across my body, making me shiver, then felt the wind brush over me again and again, each time compressing my aura further and further. I felt the way my ward worked for what seemed to be hours but was only long minutes before my aura stabilized.

"What did you do?" Alexa said when I refocused on her.

"I concentrated my aura and hid the ring underneath it," I explained. "What does it feel like?"

Alexa regarded me with her head cocked before she answered. "Like I'm standing in the clear on a hot sunny day, feeling the sun beating down on me. Like a warm wind is blowing across my skin, but it's not really a wind."

"Huh. Almost poetic."

Alexa sniffed, then looked around before she asked softly, "Lily?"

"She's fine." I laughed bitterly. "An explosion would do nothing to her. She's already back in the ring, but we can't have her out."

"Why?"

"Her aura, when she's out. It'd tear through these wards," I said, gesturing about. "I'm going to have to inlay some proper wards and craft some suppression material to keep her hidden."

Alexa nodded then made a face. "I'm sorry. I didn't think they'd act so fast."

"Not your fault. You warned me. Not to rely on them. Not to keep putting things off. I just... I didn't want to believe they'd give up on me, on us, that easily."

Alexa flashed a sad smile, and I couldn't help but remember that she had been discarded. Perhaps I should have listened to her. Too late. Too damn late.

And now here we were, hunkered in a storage space, hoping the artifacts I'd created would work. Would be enough. But even now, I felt the strain placed on the wood around my neck, the way it had already begun to crumble. It wouldn't give away immediately, but eventually. Eventually...

"Now what?" Alexa said.

I closed my eyes before opening them again. "Let's grab what's useful here. Then we should get moving. I'll cast a dispersal spell, try to hide our exit. But we should get moving across water and fast. Out of this city preferably."

Alexa nodded. "I've got a place. And some funds set aside. We'll just need to make a quick stop."

By this point, I was too tired to be surprised by her words. In the end, all I felt was gratitude that at least one of us had planned for this. Planned to be betrayed.

***

"A bowling alley?" I said, raising an eyebrow at Alexa.

Once we left the storage center, we'd wandered around for a few hours, taking a ferry ride across the bay then back again, muddying our trail. It wasn't perfect, but it was better than nothing. After that, Alexa had taken the lead, first to a co-working space where we chilled for a few hours in a rented office before we finally arrived at the bowling alley as it opened.

"This way," Alexa said, leading me straight to the storage lockers.

I twigged onto the concept fast enough and followed, casting glances around to make sure we weren't watched. Unsurprisingly, the staff—made up of horny and bored teenagers—had little care for us.

Alexa pulled a large duffel bag from the storage locker and changed out her jacket for one that was within before she pushed the duffel at me. I frowned, opening it, before my jaw dropped.

"Where'd you get that?" I said.

"Took it," Alexa said.

Within the now-open bag was a casting wand, a smaller version of the staff I'd been forced to leave behind. I blinked, staring at the wand, and remembered how I'd tossed it aside due to my dissatisfaction with the placement of the wards and then couldn't find it. I'd lost nearly an hour searching the house for it before finally giving up, figuring I'd find it hidden beneath a couch cushion or stuck underneath my bed. Or on top of the bookcase, because that made *sense* when I put it there. But now, here it was.

I picked up the wand, frowning in consternation as I noticed numerous flaws. I'd made this nearly half a year ago, and I'd grown in ability and skill since then. Enough so that the mistakes I'd made were clearly evident with even a simple perusal. My fingers itched to fix them, but I pushed it aside and slipped the wand into my jacket. Not that I needed it, but like my staff, the wand could take over casting aspects—just not as many my staff.

I also took a bundle of cash, sliding it into my jacket after peeling off a few bills for my wallet. I didn't ask how Alexa had managed to squirrel away this much. It really wasn't my business. I was just grateful that she had done so. What was surprising was the set of fake IDs within, all in a Ziploc bag.

"Fake IDs?" I said, raising an eyebrow.

"Yes. Change them out quickly. We should leave the city when we can," Alexa replied.

"About that… how?" I said. "I don't think public transportation is smart, and it's not as if we can get a rideshare. Not without our phones."

"Got it sorted," Alexa said. "Relax."

I frowned but took her word for it, taking the proffered baseball cap and sliding it onto my head. Well, she was the expert in this. My expertise with disguise mostly consisted of pixels, rooftops, and killing the guards who found you sneaking by.

***

Three hours later, we were seated in the luxurious comfort of polyester cushions, colored a dirty grey and green, a black plastic divider between us and a LCD screen to entertain us in front. Cold air blew from overhead, doing little to drown out the loud grey-haired retirees making new friends and speaking of the next "attraction" they were going to see.

I muttered to Alexa, "A tour bus? Your great plan is a tour bus filled with retirees?"

"Yes," Alexa said, looking all kinds of smug. "Public transportation, but not really. The windows are all shaded, so there's no way for people to see inside. Tours like these run every day of the week, going to multiple locations. And unless they're doing full checks of the bus, even traffic stops won't matter."

I had to admit, the woman was right. Most traffic stops would never board a bus, especially not on any of the major highways. The kind of delay that would create would only happen in the worst-case scenarios, and I didn't think our opponents had that kind of influence.

Which meant…

"I'm assuming we're not going to stay for the whole tour?" I said.

"No. We'll change out three cities out, but for tonight…" She waved around the bus. "We'll sleep through the night here and be out of the city."

"As if I could sleep," I said, which made Alexa smile slightly.

"Well, I can. So if you're going to stay awake…"

I gestured, to which the blonde smiled and rolled up her jacket to rest her head against the window. In moments, the ex-Initiate was asleep, dead to the world, though I knew she would wake fully alert if necessary. I envied her ability sometimes.

"Might as well get to work," I muttered and fished in my bag for the crafting material. Nothing special, but with only the equipment I was wearing, I needed more tools. The carving knife and blocks of wood would get me that.

Our attackers might have driven us out of my house and nearly killed us, but that nearly would cost them. I might not know who had attacked us or why, but it didn't matter. We'd survived, and so long as we lived, we could get stronger. We could get better.

As the bus finally pulled away from the curb, its passengers fully loaded, I promised myself that I'd be back. Back to my home. Returned not in ignominious defeat but in triumph. One day.

I'd be back.

Chapter 14

"Are you ready?" Alexa asked as she stood over me.

I gave the ex-Initiate a quick nod, touching Lily's ring and sending a mental reassurance to the jinn. Four months later and we had yet to summon her. There were a dozen excuses—from needing the right materials, to prioritizing new aura blockers, to not locating a quiet enough place to do it—but in the end, it meant we had left the jinn in the ring.

I had to admit, I missed the game-addicted jinn, late-night Smash Bros duels and conversations over meals. Occasionally, when I finished a quest, she'd slipped a sentence or two into the quest notifications, but it wasn't the same. I missed my friend. But at least this way, the pair of us had a better chance of hiding.

"You know, I liked this place," I said, looking around at the small house we had rented.

We'd found the advertisement in a gas station, pasted in the window, and moved in. Once a wedding present, before the enterprising couple realized that the small house lifestyle wasn't for them, now the simple single-story, container-turned-house sat in their backyard, filled by transients like us. The rent was cheap, the amenities barebones, but it had been nice.

"It was a change from the flop-houses," Alexa said, making a face.

I flashed her a wry smile, knowing that the pretty ex-blonde had had it worse in those locations. She'd dyed her hair soon after we left the city, going for boring black, and touched up her roots every few days. But bad dye jobs and baggy clothing did little to hide her beauty.

"But we can't stay. You know that."

"I know. The dice said eleven days, so eleven it is," I said.

Rather than fall into any recognizable pattern, we'd chosen to stay where we could, when we could, based off dice rolls. We limited ourselves to a maximum of twelve days in any one location. Even our next destination was a roll of the dice, public transportation and small towns our go-to choices.

Hefting the backpack, I slid it on. We closed the door, left the key in the mailbox, and headed out into cold autumn weather. Luckily, we'd been trending south for the most part, staying in warmer climates by roll of dice and choice. We'd debated long and hard about moving into another big city or sticking to small towns before we decided to leave it to chance. Our enemies were varied and numerous, and there were no good choices.

Big cities had teeming masses of people, enough that we could get lost in the anonymity of the populace. On top of that, big cities had a wide variety of cash-only jobs, the kinds that we survived on these days. In a pinch, we could mug and steal from the local drug dealer or pimp, taking their illicit gains for our own before departing town. Of course, we'd only done that twice. While criminals might not make police reports, they were prone to gossip. And guns that don't fire, sudden disorientations and fatigue, and a highly-skilled female martial artist beating the crap out of them with a pair of sticks were the kind of rumors we didn't want spreading.

For all those advantages, big cities had higher concentrations of supernaturals, increasing the odds of randomly running into someone dangerous. On top of that, big cities were the centerpiece of our surveillance state. There were few areas we could go in a major city without having our faces recorded. And my new mustache, a ball cap, and a pair of contact lenses was a poor disguise, even if it was supplemented by magic.

Small towns, on the other hand, substituted technological busybodies with human irritants. The number of inquisitive neighbors we met—especially those who were surprised by our mixed-race relations in certain smaller towns—was staggering. It had gotten so bad that I'd used glamour spells to alter my race at times, just to avoid the questions.

On top of that, smaller towns and out-of-town cottages offered little in terms of employment or other amenities. With our resources extremely tight, we couldn't afford to stay in such places long before we had to move on, looking for work where we could. And rather annoyingly, smaller towns also often had their local guardians—pagan magicians, shamans, or local supernaturals. Even if they didn't desire to be involved in the politics of the greater supernatural community, we only needed a single one of them to put together the clues and report us.

"Do you think we've managed to lose them?" I said, cocking my head toward Alexa.

The town before, we'd been attacked. A group of journeyman Mages, bearing the symbols of the Mage Council—though probably not directly commanded to—had located us. We'd left their corpses and a destroyed neighborhood behind, stealing their belongings and funds before driving for two days straight.

"Maybe," Alexa said, weariness in her voice.

I saw the bags under her eyes, the tension in her shoulders, and I winced. She walked to the junker we'd picked up, dropped her bag in the back, and got in even as I hurried to catch up. I knew how tired she was, how little sleep she took each night. The duty, the burden of our safety had fallen on her, for I was focused on the only way out we had.

Studying. And leveling.

It would be fitting to say I had grown in strength by leaps and bounds. I was now Level 76. A significant increase in strength. But it had been four months, and at this rate of increase, to meet the standards of even a single Third Circle Mage, I would need another half decade. A decade minimum to be where we needed to be for battle.

As I looked at the strained face of my friend, the bags under her eyes, then looked at my hands, I wondered. Could we last that long?

***

We were taking a small country road, driving carefully because small and underused also meant badly maintained. We were doing just under forty miles an hour after taking a turn, green vegetation from fenced-in fields all around us, some farmer's crop swaying in the wind, when the man stepped into the middle of the road. I jerked up against my seat belt as Alexa braked, instincts overriding caution as we screeched to a stop a bare foot away from hitting him. The car fish-tailed slightly as Alexa tried to dodge him at the same time.

Turning my head sideways, I regarded the man standing in the center of the road, hands on a small cane. He was dressed in a simple green cotton jacket, sleeves rolled up on tanned skin, light brown hair close-cropped. When he smiled, the wrinkles around his eyes deepened, showcasing the lack of chemical injections to his face and his advanced-sixtyish age. My eyes narrowed when Lily flashed a Status notification.

Julian Barber (Level 218)
HP: 3100/3100
MP: 0/0

None of that told me who he was, but the lack of Mana signature, the lack of magic was a relief. His level, on the other hand, wasn't, and I had to wonder how he was that high-leveled and still not a Mage. The ridiculous hit points was a clue of course. A very pointed one.

"Mage Tsien. Ms. Dumough," Barber called, tapping the cane on the ground. "Do not flee. It will not help. I am here to speak only."

Alexa growled, backing the car a bit and straightening it out. She never took her eyes off Barber as she angled the vehicle to go around him, all the while trusting me to safeguard us. When she was finally happy, she reached down beside her seat and picked up the pistol, aiming it at Barber while keeping it hidden. Only then did I roll down the window.

"Talk," Alexa said.

Now that Alexa had her attention on him fully, I cast a quick Detection spell, a variation on the Scry & Observe spell that I had known so long ago. This one was a Detect Life spell whose gain was set to just a little higher than a squirrel. As the spell washed out, details flickered through my mind. A couple of crows and Barber were the only ones present in the five-hundred-yard radius the spell gave good data on. Outside of that, returned data broke down, but even there, the area around us was relatively clear of major life-forms.

"I have a message for you." The cane rose, making the pair of us tense. But it was not an attack, just a pointer. "The Mage, that is."

"What's the message?" Alexa said. Softer, her eyes never moving from Barber. "I've heard of him. He's a famous tracker. Lycanthrope."

I swore and almost missed what Barber said next.

"You have until the new year. If you do not return to the city by then, they will kill your mother. And one more for every month you continue to hide."

I shuddered, his words making me break out into a sweat. My family… my sister… What? How? For a time, my mind went blank, unable to process the threat so casually delivered.

"You can't!" Alexa said angrily. "They're not part of this. Not of our world. They're mundanes! The law—"

"Tradition can be broken. Will be broken." Barber made a face. "I am sorry. I am just one of many messengers. What they are doing, I do not agree with. But if you did not receive this message, they would have carried out their threats anyway. Those who want you dead are not the kind to offer clemency or extensions."

"Why end of the year?" I croaked, my mind latching onto the portion that had surprised me.

"A compromise. You have done well, hiding. There was some concern you would dodge all the messengers."

I grunted, my mind casting back to my mother, my sister. To those I'd left behind. I'd forgotten about them, forgotten they'd be vulnerable too. I should have thought of it, should have known. Should have…

"Is that all?" Alexa said, glaring at Barber.

When he stepped away from the car and nodded, Alexa floored the vehicle, taking us away from him. No longer caring about potholes or sudden cows, she took us away. All while I considered my failure.

***

We didn't stop for hours. We crossed half the state and ended up in another broken-down motel, paying in cash for a pair of beds that I cast Cleanse on the moment I finished setting up our protective wards. In the meantime, Alexa verified that the room wasn't bugged before snatching the keys and doing another check on the car. Not that she hadn't done that hours ago, but we were somewhat paranoid. Half an hour later, we'd done all we could to ensure that we weren't tracked and were seated across from one another on worn, if now clean, beds as an old cathode ray television played in the background.

"I have to go back." I broke the silence, facing the truth head-on. Stating what I knew had to be said, even though I knew it was the wrong choice. The expected choice.

"I know."

"You shouldn't try to convince me—" I paused as my brain caught up with me. "You're not going to argue with me?"

Alexa let out a bark of laughter that cut-off. "No. They are threatening your family. I would be disappointed if you chose not to go."

"Even if it might be a bluff?"

"Can you risk it being a bluff?" Alexa asked. When she saw the look on my face, she continued. "That is why it is such an effective threat."

"I should have…" I drew a deep breath, settling my emotions even as I pushed aside the need to explain, to make excuses. It was too late to tell the truth. To warn my family. To do something different. Yet I could not help but feel the gnawing guilt in my stomach, the pain from putting people I loved in danger. But I could not have given up Lily either. Not to be used, abused, for ages.

"It isn't your fault," Alexa said softly. "You never had a good choice."

"But maybe I could have trusted them. They asked. Begged me to trust them." I turned away and wiped my eyes. "Now they might die."

"They won't," Alexa said firmly. "We'll go back and we'll make sure they're safe."

"We?"

"You're not getting rid of me that easily," Alexa said.

"I can't ask you to do this."

"Who's asking?"

I found myself smiling in gratitude. "So. What? We go back now?"

"No. Not yet."

"But…"

"They're not going to harm them. He gave you the deadline for a reason," Alexa said, her eyes narrowing. "We have two months. Let's not rush it."

My stomach twisted, first with fear then with anger. "You can't be sure they won't act before then."

"And you can't be sure they won't hurt your family if you don't give them Lily," Alexa snapped. "There's only one ring, remember? What if you went there and they fought over the ring? What if the group that didn't get it wanted to take it out on your family? Or they tried to make you give it to them first by taking your family first?" When I had no answer, Alexa continued. "You don't know what the status of your family is. Are they captured? Are they just watched? I assume they're watching them, but what if I'm wrong? We don't even know who 'them' is. Not really."

"But it was the…" I fell silent. I had no idea who was threatening my family. I assumed it was the Mage Council, because… I wasn't even sure why. Because they were the ones I thought had been following me? But they weren't the ones who'd launched the first attack. After all, they had a way in back then. I'd just assumed. This entire thing was really getting to me.

"Exactly. They didn't even give you a specific time or place. Just the city. So what does that tell you?" Alexa said, her voice quieter now, no longer as forceful as I'd calmed down.

"I'm… not sure."

"Neither am I. But I think we should find out, don't you?" When I reluctantly nodded, Alexa smiled at me. "Tomorrow, we'll split up."

"Huh?"

"You can't find out what's going on. And it's obvious that together, we're targets. So we'll split up. You train and Level. I'll find out what's going on in the city."

"You?" I let my eyes rake over the statuesque woman. "Alexa, you're… ummm…"

"Less noticeable than a Mage with his magic aura? Trained in espionage? With knowledge and contacts in the supernatural world—especially in the city—over and above yours? And most importantly, not the most wanted man on Earth?" Alexa said.

"But you're known."

"I'll avoid our enemies. But the man on the street? The ones we've helped? They won't care. They won't even know. It's not as if the organizations are going to announce that they're hunting you. Not exactly the kind of news they want to spread around. Bad for their reputations in some cases. Dangerous in others," Alexa said.

Acting against me exposed organizations that might not want me to survive long enough to become a power to their enemies. It was one of the reasons the Mage Council had been willing to watch over me—a way to act against their enemies without expending significant resources. If the Council wasn't acting against me directly, nor the Orders, Alexa was safer. At the very least, she wasn't the final target. And we did need that information.

Still…

"Why are you doing this?" I said, tilting my head sideways as I regarded the ex-Initiate. "This, this is a lot more than what a friend can be expected to do."

"Friend… I guess so." Alexa offered me a half-smile. "But I don't think you're just a friend. You're family. And if I've learnt anything, family means giving everything."

"Without hope or expectation of anything in return." My lips twisted into another wry smile before I decided to admit it. It was the least I could do. "I think of you as family too. You and Lily."

Alexa flashed me a smile, then leaned forward as she explained her plan. I'd be surprised that she had one, but after so many years and hours of driving, I wasn't. If anything, sometimes I wondered if Lily should have gone to Alexa. Certainly she was better at planning and figuring things out than I was. All I had was a little knowledge from my gaming days.

Pushing aside guilt and my need to control things, I focused. Because my feelings didn't matter here, and more importantly, it wasn't just my life on the line anymore. Not even just Alexa's. Now it was about my entire family, and I would not fail them. No matter what.

Chapter 15

Twelve hours later, I was standing in the basement of a rented farmhouse. The farmhouse was one of those incongruities of the modern age—a building that had once housed the farmer and his family, now abandoned as pieces of a once-proud farm had been sold off in dribs and drabs until nothing more than a large field was available. Unsuited for a working farm now, it functioned as a country retreat for rich yuppies and the occasional tourist. Like me.

Of course, the homeowner had been surprised when I turned up alone, carrying nothing more than a single backpack, to take the entire location for myself. But once I handed him the month's rent up front in cash, questions had disappeared.

Once I was settled in, I had to clear out the basement and set up multiple repeating wards. I kept at it, layering ward after ward till I was fairly certain that between the wards and the ambient interference from a nearby ley line, I should be safe.

My hand hovered over my ring as I stood in the middle of the enchanted circle, my wards glowing, the entire basement lit by a quartet of fluorescent bulbs. If I was wrong, I'd be setting a flare off for everyone and their hellhounds to find me. But if I didn't…

Tired of my own hesitation, I rubbed the ring, sending a thought beckoning Lily out. At first there was nothing, and then… there was nothing. Frowning, I stared at my ring, wondering if I had broken it. Her. Then I discarded the thought for being silly.

"You're risking a lot," Lily spoke up and made me jump.

I turned toward her. Seated to the side of me, legs crossed, Lily tilted her head as she regarded my form.

"I had to."

"Your family."

"You heard?" I sighed. "Of course you heard. You're always around."

"I'm sorry. I wish… I wish we had thought of that."

"Covered them with the wish or something?" I said, grimacing. I should have thought of that. I should have… "Can I wish them away?"

"Your family?" Lily raised an eyebrow. "It's doable, but—"

"No, not them. My enemies. Can I wish them dead?" I said, anger heating my voice.

"All of them?" Lily's voice grew quieter.

"Yes!"

"And how'd you define enemy?"

"Those threatening my family. Those threatening Alexa. And me," I said.

"The entire organization?" Lily asked softly.

"Yes!"

"All of those organizations?"

"*Yes!*"

"Is that your wish? Your final wish? Master." Lily's voice grew cold, distant, and officious. It was enough to make me pause, to stare at her.

"Nooo…" I whispered, closing my eyes. "No. I'm not going to ask you to kill hundreds—"

"Thousands."

"Thousands for my-my peace of mind." I sighed and carefully stepped out of the containment circle, then sat on a dusty chair. I coughed a little, clearing my throat, and cast a grasping hand to float over a bottle of water. After taking a swig, I looked back at Lily, my lips twisting in a wry smile. "Sorry about that."

"For almost making me become a mass murderer again?" Lily said.

"Again?"

Lily looked sad, a hand fiddling with a stray lock of hair. "Dark history, remember?"

I nodded. For all that she had played fair with me, with the ring, if she had been given that kind of order before, she'd have no choice. Never mind whatever else she might have done before her imprisonment. "Yeah. Sorry. Could you have done it?"

Lily paused, cocking her head. Her eyes grew distant, weighing the lives and deaths of thousands before she shrugged. "Eventually. If you managed to stay alive and hidden long enough. But probably not."

"I'm not sure if I'm relived or sad about that," I said.

Lily let out a choked laugh before she fell silent, staring at me.

Eventually, I grew uncomfortable enough to ask, "What?"

"You've changed. Grown more serious."

"Being chased around the country has a tendency to do that," I said.

"Also, you're the one who summoned me. Did you have something in mind?"

"I need to Level up," I said. "I need to increase my strength. I need to learn, to get better."

"You intend to fight them?" Lily said, frowning.

"Not exactly. I think, I think I need to be a distraction. For Alexa to get my family out. And then while they're chasing me and the ring, then I'll need to escape too."

"Another portable shelter?"

"No. They'll be ready for that." I drew a deep breath before letting it out, resolve growing stronger in my voice. "I need to hurt them. Make them think twice about angering me. I need to be a credible threat."

"In two months?" Lily raised an arched eyebrow.

"Yeah." I knew how crazy that sounded. How impossible that request was. I didn't need the jinn to say it.

And thankfully, she didn't. The jinn just nodded before cracking her head to the side. "Then let's get to work."

***

How do you raise Levels fast? As any gamer knows, you grind. In my case, since my Levels were tied into my magical understanding and my body's ability to channel magic, I spent hours casting spells. Making adjustments in the spell formulas, pushing my understanding and abilities to the maximum. I cast spells while upside down, while blindfolded, without moving my hands, with only oral components or even without that. Spells were formed and created, mixed and matched with reckless abandon.

Again and again, the shielding spells I created—and recreated—in the basement were put to the test as my headlong rush toward enlightenment had explosive consequences. I burnt my eyebrows off twice, my hair four times before I gave up and shaved it tight. I picked up myriad scars on my hands, the Mana channels in my fingers and palms burnt and scarred from spell blowback. Late into the night, I trained, falling asleep on the table only to wake from the throbbing pain as my exhausted Mana channels protested the abuse. Only for me to start again.

Not that I didn't take care to not over-exhaust myself. I took expeditions, Quests that Lily offered as she stretched the boundaries of the ring to the maximum. A dryad's healing sap, taken from her tree after helping her with a logging problem from the local forestry company, put into a bath helped to fix some of the burgeoning problems. A local group of giant beavers needed their dam reinforced, the natural enchantments around the dam no longer sufficient to stop queries from the locals. A Chupacabra infestation killed off.

Those were the easier quests. Other, more dangerous ones saw me stumbling home, bleeding from wounds, my clothing and armor shredded. Victorious while fighting the monsters in the dark. Wendigos. Wraiths. Other darker, unspeakable creatures that lurked at the edges of civilization, waiting for the foolish, the unwary. Normally they'd be impossible to find without help, without significant time invested. But I had a cheat—I had a friend who could find them and give me their locations. And she let me throw myself at them, all in a bid to let me learn. Learn new and painful ways to stay alive.

But monsters were not all that I hunted. In two cases, I ambushed hunting parties, individuals searching for me. I ended their lives before they could get too close, before they could locate me. It was dangerous, going hours away in different directions to attack them, to leave trails. But it was necessary. For my training. For my safety.

Days passed, days of sweat and pain. It ended a month and a half later when my burner phone, kept turned off but for five minutes a day, beeped with a waiting message.

Meet in 5. Purple Green—Z

It was in code, a simple one that we'd agreed on. Three locations, each given a color. The time was in days—not five days as the number mentioned, but seven. Add two to the number offered. And the name was a simple transliteration, a shift of the alphabet. Z meant A—Alexa. But Z also meant she was doing this unencumbered, unthreatened.

A tension that I had not known that I carried released, the knowledge that my friend was fine relieving a little bit of my worry. But I sobered up soon after, knowing that the hard part was coming next. The bad part.

"Is it time?" Lily said from her corner.

I looked at where my friend sat patiently. Trapped in a circle, forced to stay there lest she let the world know where she was. Lest she bring their wrath upon us. More than what had been brought at least. One and a half months, and she had never voiced a single complaint. Not a request for a cell phone to play a game on, not a single whine about how bored she was. Every moment, every time we spoke, she had helped as best she could, pushing the boundaries of the enchantment, of the rules set upon her. Disregarding the pain to help. To help me.

"Yes," I said.

Steps took me over, and I stared at Lily, the jinn who had brought both wonder and terror to my life. Who had supported me while I threw myself into danger, all the while shackled to me and my life. I drew a deep breath, then let it out, trying to find the words.

"You don't have to say it. I'm ready. While you were out questing, before this"—Lily gestured around the dank basement—"I was downloading and copying all the games I could get hold of. They're all in my ring. All the books, all the games. Quite a few replicas of the various game machines too. If you fail… I'll be fine."

I ducked my head then, memory of the devil's deal we made pushing against my soul, my guilt. If I failed—when I failed and died—Lily would be forced to an eternity of solitude. Trapped by the ring, trapped forever by her own power.

"It's fine. The ring itself is failing. Another ten thousand years, I'm sure I'll be able to break free," Lily said with false cheer.

After so long, even I knew she was being optimistic. The greatest failure point in her ring was the material itself, but even that would take tens of thousands of years to break down. After all, the enchantment took a portion of her strength to bolster the durability of the ring.

"I-I wasn't thinking that," I said. Lily made a mocking hurt face and I felt my lips twitch. "Stop it. This is serious."

"Deadly serious."

I stared at the jinn incredulously before breaking into laughter, shaking my head. "Gods. You're impossible."

"Yup. That's why I'm stuck in here."

That kept me laughing until even Lily broke down and joined me. Together, we laughed until I had to wipe the tears away.

"Thank you. I think I needed that," I said.

"Almost as much as you need getting laid."

"Ugh. Don't remind me," I said and tugged at my jeans. Living with two beautiful women, neither of which I was sleeping with, had been hard. Especially when my social life had become non-existent. Hell, even when I was penniless and a hardcore gamer, I'd gotten better action. "And stop distracting me. I was trying to say thank you. And sorry."

"You don't have to." Lily placed a hand over her heart, looking me in the eyes. "This. This has been the best time of my life."

"Not a high bar, with the masters you've had before."

"No. Not just while I've been enslaved. In my life." Lily intoned those words with assurance. "You treated me like—like a friend. You let me stay out. You let me play games. You didn't push me when I had problems with going out. And then did, when I needed it. You listened to me and laughed with me. You and Alexa, you've offered me…" I waited for her to finish, but she did not. Instead, she flashed me a smile. "Thank you."

"No, I should—I'm talking to air." I sighed as the jinn disappeared, having gone back to her ring. There was no warning, no flash of light. One second she was there, the next she was gone. Except she wasn't really gone. I touched the ring again, twisting it on my finger. "I still think I owe you. And if I survive, we'll go find some of those augmented reality places and play them as much as you want."

I could almost swear I heard a squeal of excitement rise from the ring. Smiling, I turned away and began the process of packing up. Time to get ready to go.

***

Three hours later—one of which consisted of cleaning up the various enchantments and the other two of hiking into town—I was footsore and tired, waiting at the bus depot for the next cross-country coach. Traveling by coach into the city was neither glamorous nor smart, which was why our meeting point was not in the city itself. Still, the bus was convenient and cheap—and considering I had just spent the vast majority of my liquid funds, the last was highly important.

The bus stop was shaded from the midday sun and open to the elements otherwise. That left me shivering as winter winds blew through the single-road town. Magic could have solved the problem, but I was too close to my goals to break discipline. No more magic, not till the city. I couldn't afford to let them know, not now.

"Nice bag." A teenager on his skateboard kicked it up, marveling at my duffel. It had been purchased from an army surplus store, at first an ugly camo green, but now bedecked with gold and red thread. The gold shimmered slightly as it caught rays of light and the kid's attention. "Love the style, man. Peace and war."

"Thanks." I looked down, spotting the hippie peace symbol that had caught the kid's attention before shrugging. "You know what they say."

"What?"

"Hope for peace, prepare for war."

"Deeeep." The teenager nodded and let the board down, waving goodbye as he kicked off. "Later!"

Thankfully the kid hadn't queried about why the thread was glowing and shimmering. Residual magicfrom the enchanted objects within was bleeding off, too much magic in too close a place. The runic designs could barely suppress the magical signature, so the physical signs were a trade-off I had to make. If I'd had more time, if I'd had better materials...

If, if, if.

But I had no more time for ifs. At least, not for those in the past. The future, the potential ifs, those I had time for. Those I had planned for.

With the many, many enchanted objects I'd made. And *if* I had the opportunity, maybe I'd be able to really show them what it meant to anger a gamer.

Chapter 16

"If I survive this, I'm never staying in another dingy motel," I said when Alexa walked in seven days later.

It had taken me two days to make it to our meeting spot, after which I'd ended up staying in a motel room, finishing up the last of my preparations. Most of that consisted of repeatedly making the same enchantments I had made before, carving new wards and enchantments into whatever materials I could get my hands on. Getting ready.

"They do have a certain disreputable character to them," Alexa said, wrinkling her nose. "Did you know, when I asked about the key you left for me, the receptionist winked at me. As if I was… I was…"

"Doing something illicit?"

"Yes!"

"Well, we kind of are…"

"Not like that!" Alexa said, looking scandalized. "I would never. Especially with you!"

"I'm hurt," I said, clutching my chest.

Alexa smacked the top of my head and I laughed. I stopped the moment she dropped a thick file folder on the bed.

"My family?" I said.

"Alive. Unharmed. And untouched. They don't seem to know what's going on, though they are worried about you."

I breathed a sigh of relief, grateful for all that she had said. But… "Worried?"

"Yes. They've even lodged a missing person's report."

"Shit." I breathed deeply and shook my head. Surely that wasn't as bad as I thought. Getting rid of a missing person's report should be simple. I was an adult. I could disappear for no good reason. After my house burned down… "Hundred hells' worth of shit."

"Just about." Alexa said. "Good thing you changed your hairstyle. You don't look at all like the photo they have of you on the missing person's report. It's, like, six years out of date. Also, I like the spikes."

I ran a hand across my hair, feeling the spikey and now blond-tipped hair. It was a little eye-catching, but not much. Add a pair of glasses that I didn't need and bulky shirts and it was an easy change of appearance. As for the photo… six years? Had I not stayed for a photo, not taken one with my family for that long? In an age of selfies and mobile phones, of Facebook and Instagram, how had they not had a better photograph?

"Henry?" Alexa said, drawing my attention as she opened the file. "Are you with me?"

"Yes. Go on," I said.

"Okay. Here's what I found…"

***

Debriefing took hours. Not just because there was so much information to get through, but because

I had questions. So many questions. I did my best to keep them on track, but questions about how she'd gotten all this information, what she'd had to do to get it abounded. Something in the way Alexa spoke, the way she held herself, the lines under her eyes and the pain in them told me I might not like the answers. And so I didn't ask, even if I wanted to.

"All right. So, to sum up. We need to get my family out in two days—Saturday—because that's when all my family will be in one place. They'll be watching more than ever, but you're hoping I can pull at least some of their people off. Because otherwise, there's too many," I said, my eyes narrowing. "That sum up that portion?"

"Yes."

"As for threats we're facing, we've got…" I took a deep breath and exhaled threadily. "The Dark Council. A small faction of the fey. At least four different Knightly Orders. Two different mundane hunter organizations. A naiad bounty hunting group. And a group of Oni gangsters."

"Those are the credible threats. There are more, but those are the ones you have to worry about. I want you to memorize their pictures and details." Alexa tapped the pile of files she'd drawn from her bag as we'd been talking. I'd glimpsed the details, but she was right. Knowing what they looked like would help. "Now, what were you up to?"

I found myself grinning, pulling up the duffel bag and plopping it onto the bed. Then I pushed against the bundle of Mana that made up my Level stats and made it visible to Alexa. "Why don't you check it out yourself?"

Class: Mage
Level 79 (11% Experience)
Known Spells: Elemental Control (4 Base, Force), Mana Control, Shaped Control, Forced Healing, Heal, Wards, Link, Track, Wards, Greater Glamour & Illusion, Lesser Summoning, Empower, Lesser Divination, Cleanse, Runic Script, Elemental Resistances.

"This is rather different." Alexa frowned as she looked over my adjusted spell list. "You're missing a lot."

"We decided to clean things up," I said. "Once I'd progressed my Elemental Control, I didn't really need a slot for Iceball, Fireball, Airball, or Earthball and then another one for each type of dart, spear, cone, or whatever else I decided to come up with. Part of my training was learning to deconstruct spells so that I'm just shaping the elements to make it what I need."

"Makes sense. Doesn't tell me what you can do though."

"Pretty much everything you've seen me do, except bigger. I can link two different elements together now, so I can generate a Firestorm or create a Freezing Fog without relying on the spell formula's Lily put in my head. Magma's a bit out of my wheelhouse and Lily refuses to teach me that one," I said, pouting a little. "But my biggest improvement is in my actual skill set. Here…"

Another mental prod and a new piece of data appeared.

Magical Skill Set
*Mana Flow: 7/10 **
Mana to Energy Conversion: 6/10
Spell Container: 8/10
Spatial Location: 6/10
Spatial Movement: 6/10
Energy Manipulation: 6/10
Biological Manipulation: 4/10
Matter Manipulation: 7/10
Summoning: 2/10
Duration: 7/10
Rituals: 2/10
Multi-Casting: 6/10
Enchanting: 8/10

"Your spell container and enchanting abilities are really up there, aren't they?" Alexa said.

"Yup. Have to be. They feed into one another. Got to control the inscribed runes when I'm enchanting, so that's been progressing along with the matter manipulation. Same with multi-casting, though I've hit a wall there," I said. "When I'm enchanting, I can handle up to eight different flows. But once I start moving and fighting, I drop down to about four. Five at a push."

"Five spells?" Alexa's eyebrow rose in surprise.

"Five flows. Three to four spells, depending on how complicated the spells are and if I'm using a pre-generated one or not," I clarified.

"Oh. Right." Alexa fell silent, and I basked in her good regard, knowing that my month and half of struggle and pain had resulted in great improvements. When I stayed silent, Alexa frowned. "And the asterisk?"

"What asterisk?"

"That one!"

I frowned and looked closer, then blinked. "That wasn't there… *Lily*!" Of course the jinn didn't answer me. Couldn't. I glared at my ring instead until a tap on my thigh made me look at Alexa. "It's… nothing. Just a little reminder."

"About?"

"I had to raise my Levels. So I kind of—"

"Damaged some of your Mana channels and your body?" Alexa finished for me, flicking her gaze to my scarred hands.

"If you knew, why'd you ask?" I crossed my arms, hiding my hands belatedly.

"I wanted to see if you'd tell me."

"Gah! You're as bad as my mum!" I said. Then paused, realizing what I'd said.

We both sobered, the reminder making me sigh.

"I'm looking forward to meeting her," Alexa offered into the silence.

A thought struck me. I raised a finger, then lowered it slowly.

"What?" Alexa said.

"Nothing."

"Henry…"

"Ugh. She just might want to know who you are. It's not like we, you know, introduced you or Lily," I said. "And well, she knows of you. And might, you know, think you're my girlfriend. Or something." The last was squeaked out.

"Or something?"

"Well… we have been staying together. In the same house. And my mum's wanting me to… well, you know how old people are. Parents…" I coughed, flushing red.

Alexa blushed too when she caught on, smacking me on the thigh before turning aside. After a moment, when the blush had reduced, she turned back to me. "That… might be better."

"What!?!"

"I need them to come with me. Without question," Alexa pointed out. "Them thinking we're… together might make it easier."

"Right. Right. And we can just tell them otherwise. Later," I said, running a hand through crusty hair with a grimace. "That'll be fine."

"You don't sound convincing."

"That's because it's my parents," I whined.

Alexa gave me a half-smile and I shook my head, pushing it aside. Not the time for that.

"So, wanna see my toys?" I pointed at the duffel while hefting my smaller backpack too.

"Yes!" Alexa said, almost bouncing in eagerness. There was a flash of avarice in her eyes, but more wonder. Even after all this time, the ex-Initiate still found some wonder in our lives. I wished I could mirror that right now, but…

"All right. So first, my vest." I pulled out the simple buckled-on vest that I'd mashed together from a vest and a bunch of leather cords and pouches.

"Ugly."

"I never said I was a seamstress. Or fashionista," I retorted but had to admit, the brown and green leather straps and pouches clashed with the black base of the vest. In each of the pouches was an easily accessible wooden sphere a little smaller than a baseball. "Each pouch is linked to a pouch in the duffel. I've got more copies of each of these enchanted spheres in there. So all I need to do is pull one out." I demonstrated by pulling the sphere. "Arm it and toss, and while I'm doing that…"

"It fills up!" Alexa's jaw dropped. "That's amazing. You've got an automatic replicator. But how far…?"

"About a mile. I've got multiple smaller bags with the same kind of enchantment in the duffel too, with smaller ranges. So I can basically drop the smaller bags around beforehand, giving me multiple caches to run to—but with shorter range—or I run around a central area, pulling from the duffel as necessary," I said. "Gives me options."

"What do the spheres do?"

"Basically, they're magical grenades." I pointed at each of the four pouches in turn. "Fire. Ice. Wind and earth—dust storm basically—and force sphere."

"Force sphere?"

"This one takes a little more work, but I can either make it a defensive ward—though it holds me still—or a giant wrecking ball to throw at people. There's a weird interaction between speed and size. Seems like it keeps the same momentum even when the force sphere activates, so if you throw it hard enough, it's like a wrecking ball. I have a couple for you that are pre-charged."

Alexa grinned. "That's pretty good. How many do you have?"

"For myself? About a half dozen of each type. I've also got six wands," I said, pulling out the bundle of sticks and pointing at the holsters. "Same thing, but they're attached to this bag. They don't fire more than a half-dozen overcharged attacks before they're done, but they've all got their own charges, so it won't use my Mana."

"You're planning on a long fight."

"Yup. Got a couple of enchanted masks too, pre-set glamours and illusions." I drew a breath and let it out. "I can provide the distraction. But even if you get out…"

"You're worried they'll still be caught?"

"Yeah."

"Don't worry," Alexa said. "I worked something out."

"What?"

Alexa didn't answer me. My eyes narrowed, then I realized why she didn't want to tell me. If I didn't know, it couldn't be plucked from my mind. They couldn't be used to hurt me, make me give up the ring. Though if I was already captured, would they really care about any of my friends or family?

Ah hell. Better to be safe than sorry.

"I've got a few more things." I opened the duffel and showed her the tools I'd made. An assortment of pre-set wards, enchanted blocking wards, a couple of balls of grease, a couple of invisibility potions, and even one short-term gliding potion. All tools to help me evade and hurt others when needed.

In the end, when the show-and-tell was done, we regarded one another over the pieces of my enchanted gear, a choking amount of tension appearing. Knowing what was coming. And yet unable to avoid it.

"Alexa…"

"Thank me after."

"I—"

"After," Alexa said with finality and stood. "Now, get reading. I'll get us food."

I watched as the former blonde, now bottled redhead, walked out, and I sighed. If I had another wish…

But that was the thing about magic. It might be magical, but it was no miracle. It couldn't fix most things. It was a tool. A versatile tool, but just another tool.

Chapter 17

On the designated day, sneaking into the city took me an hour. It mostly consisted of paying the exorbitant fees to take a taxi from the motel to Faircreek in the southwest. There, the abandoned city docks and the crumbling warehouses made for an urban maze of derelict buildings and low population numbers. Of course, depressed business district or not, it wasn't empty. Which was why I made sure to drop off and hide my duffel in an empty building before making my way to talk to an old friend.

"Wizard. Haven't seen you in a bit." Andy, the green-skinned ganger orc that ran these streets—or at least, a portion of them—greeted me with a toothy smile. "Surprised to see you here. You running another quest?"

"No," I said, shaking my head. "I don't know what you've heard—"

"Heard enough. Didn't want to believe it, but you're really in trouble, aren't you?" Andy said, deep-set eyes crinkling. "You know I'd love to help you but—"

"No need." I knew what he was going to say and also knew what he could offer. The enemies I'd made outclassed my friends by far. "But they are going to come for me. If you can get word out to get off the streets…"

"You going to fight here? In my neighborhood?" This time, there was no friendliness in Andy's voice. He reared up, glaring at me. "What the hell, wizard? Why bring your shit to us?"

"It's not on purpose. I just need—"

"Bullshit. You're choosing our place. That's very much on purpose!"

"I need a place with fewer people!" I snapped. "Or do you want me to do this in the middle of downtown?"

"Sounds great to me. Better than bringing more shit onto us." Andy pointed at me. "I thought you cared, man. But you wizards are just like the rest. Once you need to, you're just out to shit on us."

"That's not true!" I growled.

But a part of me, a nagging part, pointed out that he might have a point. I could have chosen another neighborhood. I hadn't even really considered any place else, done any research. Had I chosen a place like this because it was easier? Or was it the best choice? Even if it was the best and reduced the amount of damage to the most number of people, did heaping trouble on those who had the least make it worse?

"Get the hell out of here, wizard. And don't show your face again," Andy said, shoving my shoulder.

I took the push and backed off, wanting to explain but realizing nothing I could say would ever justify what I intended to do.

As I backed away, Andy let off one last invective. "Every person hurt by this, it's blood on your hands."

Rather than reply, I retreated. Andy barked orders to his subordinates, people who glared at me. I hurried off, turning the corner before casting a glamour to hide my face. In short order, I was another person. I still had a lot of work to do, including scattering my other pouches around the suburb. There was no guarantee that Andy wasn't being watched, not with him being one of my few friends, but thus far, Alexa hadn't found them to be keeping an eye on him. That was why I'd risked meeting him.

As I headed away, I glanced sideways, calling forth the Quest Lily had created for me.

Quest Received: Survive for Four Hours

You have been challenged to reenter the city and make yourself available to your opponents. Failure to do so will see the death of your family. As bait, you will need to survive for four hours while Alexa brings your family to safety.

Reward: The safety of your family

Failure: Your death.

Bonus Objective 1: Each additional hour of survival ensures the increased level of safety for your family

Bonus Objective 2: Escape from your pursuers after achieving your first objective

Over the next hour and a half, I moved around the business district, breaking into abandoned warehouses and sneaking into backrooms, leaving my enchanted storage bags in those locations. Of course, just to mess things up, I also cast illusion spells on random pieces of equipment. Plastic bags, a garbage can full of rotten food, and a large pile of fecal matter were among the presents I left for my trackers.

Along the way, I dropped a number of my pre-made enchanted wards, each set to release a single burst of energy. I mostly tuned them so that they triggered when met by an aura with a high enough concentration, ensuring that your random supernatural would not likely trigger them. They were my early warning system. When they went off, I had to smile grimly from the rooftop where I'd been resting.

"Guess it's time?" I said, closing my eyes. I tapped the ring. "Lily, you might as well pop out."

"You sure?" Lily said as she appeared beside me, clad in her hoodie and slacks. She pivoted, taking in our surroundings then looking at the sky, taking in the salt-encrusted fresh air that blew in from the docks a few blocks away. She looked down, spotting the runic circle I'd drawn, and shook her head slightly. "You know they'll pick me out."

"Yeah. Can't have you following me, but I thought I'd say bye one last time," I said. "Can't stay too long, but… thank you."

"Good luck, Henry."

I flashed Lily a grin before hurrying down the stairs, leaving Lily and the trap behind. For a time, her signal and the ring's would seem the same.

Which would lead my enemies right to her. Of course, once I hit the bottom of the stairs, I scattered a pouchful of pepper and cayenne peppers into the air, making sure to keep a Gust spell around my body to ensure that none of it touched me. Once I'd moved away from the pepper, I inverted the spell, keeping my scent locked to my body. It made moving a little harder, but was easier than trying to mimic an entirely new scent via an illusion spell. In the open air, I was forced to redirect the gust upward, shifting my scent into a column into the air and dispersing it high above so that it would be impossible to track me that way.

Head down, ball cap on, I trotted toward my next rally point. I didn't look back, knowing there was nothing to see. Fifteen minutes later, as I lounged behind a dumpster, the ripple of my ritual circle being broken washed over the entire suburb. The emotional resonance of anger and pain was carried on the spell remnants, making me grin. The ritual circle I'd formed had liquefied the concrete then hardened it, basically dropping anyone on the roof half into the roof before reforming around them. It wouldn't kill. Probably not even maim, if they were smart about releasing themselves. But it would scare them and hurt them.

I tilted my head, letting the Gust spell I was holding around me disappear. Turning to the side, I eyed the explosive ward I'd scribed into the wall, a ward that was integrated into a simple script—"I prepared Explosive Runes this morning."

They'd wanted me in the city. So there I was. And now, I would teach them why having me there was a bad idea. Though I was careful to keep my remote attacks to harassing attacks rather than lethal ones. I wasn't about to leave the equivalent of magical land mines for kids to walk over.

*****

I was trotting up the stairs of a mostly empty office building, headed for the roof to get to the next building over, when I heard doors open beneath me. In the corner of my eyes, I noted how the timer was reading just about three hours after the start of this entire thing. The noise from below wasn't uncommon—the building wasn't entirely abandoned—but unusual enough that I poked my head over the railing. Only to see a large red, tusked face looking back at me.

"He's here!" the Oni shouted before he reached down his side.

I jerked backward and hugged the side of the wall as I ran up. A resounding boom made my ears ache and concrete chips rained down around me as the idiot opened fire. He couldn't even see me! "Asshole."

I panted as I ran up the stairs, pulling a fire sphere from my vest. I made it to the rooftop access and yanked open the door while hearing the trump of footsteps following me. Another blast, this one making my ears ache again, sent more chips scattering around me and making me nearly drop the sphere. I gripped it tighter, sending a surge of Mana into the sphere to activate it, and tossed it over the railing. It fell and I ducked out, twisting around the doorway. Flames exploded, channeled by the stairwell column into a chimney of heat and smoke. I heard screams from within the stairwell as a gust of fire heated my skin and toasted the tips of my escaped hair.

A part of me felt guilty, knowing that the creatures I'd hurt—maybe killed—were sapients. Living, thinking creatures. Then again, the asses had shot at me immediately, never even taking a moment to check that there wasn't anyone else there.

. . .

Fuck. I hadn't either.

I turned toward the staircase, taking a half-step to it, and got caught by surprise when the door slammed open. An oni, similar to the one that had shot at me but bigger, nearing seven feet tall, ducked out. The monster had to twist to get through the door, so wide that it couldn't make its way through normally. He saw me and grabbed my jacket and jerked me close.

I flailed for a second, one hand impacting against his face to try to push away. Another hand flicked and twisted, forming a shield just above the oni's hip—perfectly placed to jerk the creature to a stop as it swung its fist up toward me. The oni jerked to a stop, confused by the sudden jarring motion, even as I finished casting my second spell and sent darts of Mana and fire straight into the monster's eyes.

Eyes were small, fast-moving targets that were hard to hit. Not surprisingly, the Oni flinched as the bright light and the Mana flew toward its face, meaning that my attack left bloody, singed furrows across its visage. Eyes clenched shut in automatic reaction, the oni threw me aside. I didn't fly far though, being that I had been thrown into the rooftop access wall and bounced off the edge before landing on the concrete.

Only the impact-resistant wards in my jacket saved me from broken bones. Instead, it spread what impact it didn't absorb across my body, leaving me winded and in pain but functioning. As I rolled over, I adjusted the location and size of my Force Wall, placing it a foot above me. Just in time too, as the oni's fist crashed into my hasty shield. I felt myself pressed into the floor, the Force Shield cracking as the built-up momentum from the muscular demon nearly shattered my defense. Before he could throw another attack, I adjusted the Force Shield again.

This time around, I kept it formed as I sent it forward. Rising from the ground, it hit the oni in the chest and lower body and kept rising, even as I twisted the spell formula once more to alter its shape. From Force Wall to a giant cradle, holding the oni around its body as the spell rose, it pushed my opponent farther away from me. There was a moment of surprise before he grabbed the edges of my spell and applied his overly muscled arms to it. In seconds, the already compromised spell shattered.

A little too late. In mid-air, the oni broke my spell and fell, but by this time, momentum and his position sent it off the edge of the roof to his death.

I couldn't help but grin grimly, hobbling to the side of the office building that had been my initial objective. A hand went into a pocket and another pouch of pepper, cayenne pepper, and durian-scented candles were dumped behind me. I left the durian-scented candles burning with a gesture as I retreated to the next building's rooftop, hopping down the six-foot drop and landing with a grunt.

With all the commotion, I was sure the rest of my opponents were on their way. I had to retreat far enough that my presence was harder to locate. I kept moving even as I reformed my wind spell to keep my scent contained. I ran along the warehouse roof to the edge of where it met the next street over, then a simple glide and levitation spell combined allowed me to jump across the street while I wrapped myself in a fourth illusion spell, hiding my presence.

When I landed on the other side of the street, I crouched on the rooftop and pulled out another sphere, adjusting the activation portion of the enchantment to target any supernaturally strong aura that came within range and wasn't mine. I hoped that no one would be wandering the rooftop before daylight rose again, but it was a risk I had to take.

As I rose, halfway to my feet, I froze when I sensed other auras. Strong, powerful, supernatural auras. My lips curled up in a snarl even as I noted that my enemies weren't bothering to hide their auras. Foolish and cocky. As I scuttled away, I rebuked myself. There was no guarantee that the auras I sensed were the only ones in play.

In fact… I grew more careful, scanning the rooftops for potential dangers. If it was me, I'd use both. Hidden and visible hunters—the first to catch me unaware and the second to make me overly confident. I reminded myself that it was best to stay cautious. That this was our first encounter and it was just a start.

***

For all my mental wariness, the next group caught me by chance twenty minutes later. I was hiding behind a dumpster, only my scent-erasing spell in play. I trusted my position and the aura-dampening enchantments woven into my jacket to keep me hidden. I was waiting, counting off the seconds as the mobile electric scooter running naiads zipped away, intent on the magic explosion two streets away. An explosion that I knew was from someone tampering with one of my enchanted packages.

I was so intent on listening and counting, I hadn't noticed the Order knights, their all-too-mortal auras bypassing my wariness. I didn't notice them till the first crossbow bolt took me in the shoulder, the blessed and faith-enchanted bolt cutting through my protective jacket and twisting me around. The second bolt, targeted at my head, missed by inches as I spun about, leaving the bolt thrumming beside my face. Even as the pair of Order knights dropped their crossbows and drew pistols, I was reaching for a sphere.

Fast as I was cross-drawing the sphere, they were faster. I ignored the loud bark of their pistols, watching the bullets glance off the defensive shield that had formed around me as the backup enchantments woven into my jacket came into play. A secondary spell enchantment formed a Force Wall the moment it was pierced. It drew upon the blood I'd spilled to power it, giving it a brief but powerful surge of strength.

An underhanded toss sent the ball skittering under my shield even as the pair of Order knights took turns firing at me while splitting apart. The moment they caught sight of the sphere, they took defensive action. One twisted his hand, raising it sideways as a glowing shield came up to protect him. The other skirted backward into the cover of a dumpster. As my sphere exploded, as the pain from my shoulder made itself known, I pulled open a potion and chugged it.

A blizzard appeared in the alleyway, one that coated the area with slick ice and dropped the temperature to about -40. It bypassed silly things like faith-based shields. Admittedly, it was not the sphere I'd meant to grab, but it worked well enough. The pair of Knights came out of hiding to level their guns at me. I flashed them a smile around the edges of the sports bottle that contained my potion, then I felt the spell kick in.

Unlike my previous translocation spell, this one dropped me into the earth, displacing my body about twelve feet down. I held my breath at the last second as I dropped before I began the slow—and entirely too painful—process of swimming away. The only good news was that the bolt in my shoulder was left behind, the foreign faith enchantments on the bolt hampering my potion's ability to grip it. Unlike my bag and the rest of my equipment, it didn't have my aura engrained into it through use and magic—and while the addition of my blood might normally have dragged it along, the faith enchantments rejected the sublimation of the bolt. That meant I didn't have to try to pull it out.

It did, however, mean that I had an open wound pumping blood into the earth that surrounded me as I swam away. On top of that, I had a limited amount of time in the earth. Not due to the potion's stability—though that was, admittedly, a concern—but due to my inability to breathe. I had just about a minute before my need to add oxygen to my lungs. If I swallowed earth, it would still be in my chest when I popped back out. That would be somewhat fatal.

As I swam away, searching for an appropriately sized and distant basement, I cast a healing spell on my shoulder. It wouldn't fix my shoulder, but it would, at the least, stop the gushing blood.

***

It could be worse. I muttered that to myself constantly as I wrapped myself in glamour and illusion, the scent of my now-healed-but-still-bloody shoulder contained into small balls of concentrated air. I sent those gusting off, contained until they reached their designated locations where they would break down. If I couldn't hide my scent, then I'd overlay it all across the neighborhood to confuse the scent.

Unfortunately, business districts, especially those that used to hold a bunch of warehouses, weren't particularly known for their small, twisting streets. That meant that I had to make my way down the street in open view. As I scurried along, a cold sweat that dripped down my back made me shiver—even more so when the group of Red Caps turned the corner. One of them was leaning down, sniffing the pavement as he tried to locate me. The others scanned the street, searching for me. One even held up an old monocle. I knew the enchantment in that monocle, knew it searched for telltale portions of magic.

Dangerous, but I'd taken that into account in my own spells. Still, I had never tested the spell against another, so I felt my breathing hitch as the Red Cap looked directly at me. He paused, staring at me, at what he saw through his monocle.

"What is it?" one of the other Red Caps asked.

"Distortion."

"The Mage?" One of the Red Caps reached into his jacket, pulling out a stone throwing axe.

I felt my breath freeze.

"Not sure. Might just be another trick of his. Or one of the other hunters. Or an ambient change."

"You could be clearer!"

"This isn't science." The Red Cap growled. "It's not moving."

"I'm going to throw my axe." The Red Cap hefted the axe, making a passing car swerve slightly as the driver noted the weapon. That drew the Red Cap's attention.

The car sped up, the female driver ashen with fear.

"Careful. We don't want the damn mundanes here," the monocle-user snarled.

Before he could continue, he shifted, following a flash of darkness, a moving shadow. I tracked the motion too, but with the monocle user no longer looking at me, I reinforced my spell warding, adjusting it, and took four quick steps forward.

By the time the monocle-user looked back, I was away from my original position and hurrying down the street. "Huh."

"What?"

"It's gone."

"So?" The axe-wielder grimaced but slid his axe back into the harness under his jacket, hiding it from casual sight again.

The Red Cap group kept moving, passing on the opposite side of the road. I made myself stop, watching them pass by but doing my best not to look at them directly for fear that they'd somehow sense my attention. Only when they had passed did I scurry forward, though as I turned the corner, I thought I saw the shadow on the second floor shift again.

I frowned, tempted to check it out, but then I felt the impingement of more auras coming down the street and I groaned. Time to move. I took off as my shoulder continued to ache. Maybe drawing everyone to one business district had been a bad idea.

Perhaps I had overestimated my ability to deal with my hunters. But it really didn't matter. I had a job to do, and my friend, my family were counting on me to keep them busy. I needed to keep going for as long as I could, give Alexa time to get them to safety, to get out of the house. Everything else, from my concerns to weird shades, did not matter.

Chapter 18

I dropped through the hole in the floor, landing in a crouch, and groaned as pain shot up my knees, through my aching bum and sore back, and into my shoulder. I gritted my teeth and stood, flicking a hand upward as I drew on my Mana again. A single, clear Force Spike formed in the middle of the hole. I concentrated, making sure that it was as clear as I could make it, then I staggered over to the door, barely casting a glance at the dilapidated hotel room with its single double bed and broken dresser.

Above, my pursuers crashed through the door and set off the ice spike sphere and the air sphere. One coated the air with dust and dirt, and the second sent shards of ice forming from the floor. I heard a shriek of pain, cut off as they stumbled forward. But I stumbled out the door and headed for the staircase, hoping to lose them.

I couldn't even tell who was after me this time. The naiads? More of the orders? Not the fey. I'd killed a pair of their sidhe warriors as I was entering the building, and I didn't think they had too many pursuing me. If my pursuers weren't so intent on fighting one another—settling old scores in the chaos—they would have caught me already. As it was, my counter had switched over from a countdown to a positive number, three minutes and up. I'd passed my quest, just barely.

Ever since they caught up with me, I'd been running. Every trick in the book I had, and some that I'd come up with at the last moment, had been pulled out. I'd stood and fought, killed and butchered. Splayed their blood across a rusty playground, leaving corpses scattered by wind blades, and then hidden among the destruction to double-back. I'd drawn my pursuers into narrow alleyways and released traps to web them close. I'd burnt the trapped dhampirs. From the pursuing oni, I'd run and hid, allowing lycanthropes to smell the blood I'd planted on them, and let age-old rivalry take its turn.

And none of it mattered. I'd barely gotten more than ten minutes of rest. Constant wear had me down to four spheres. My Mana reserves, carefully husbanded, were less than a quarter full. The hotel had not been what I'd wanted to hide, but it wasn't as if I'd had a choice. When the demon dogs howled, you ran—and those sidhe had used their black hounds to push me here.

And now, I was ducking between floors, trying to find a way out that didn't lead to another fight. But there was none. Around the corner, I stumbled, only to find a tall, gangly troll staring at me. Behind him, in the shadows, a trio of creatures stood.

"You guys made it," I said wheezily. I leaned against the wall, trying to catch my breath. The scream from behind me as one of my pursuers impaled themselves on my present barely elicited a twitch.

"You have run far. But you must know how this ends." The troll's voice was urbane, civilized.

A big difference from the big, big fangs in its mouth.

I shifted a few steps away from the corner, putting myself closer to the troll, figuring I didn't want to get yanked back.

"I want to know why you're talking…" I said, cocking my head. I kept my hand low by my side as I formed a flame spear, building the container, position, and targeting options first.

"Because we have a question."

"Shoot." I inhaled further, then added, "Not literally."

"Do you have your final wish?"

I froze, some incidents clicking into place. And then…

"Take him."

I didn't see it coming. Shades came through the walls and yanked me back, smashing the back of my head into the wall. The first blow sent stars through my eyes and made my spell matrix fall apart. The second blow brought darkness even as the roaring troll and the screams of my pursuers mingled.

***

I didn't expect to wake up. After all, they were meant to kill me. End me, the ring goes away and the threat of Lily being used as a weapon was gone permanently. Waking up was a nice surprise in that sense, though the throbbing pain in my head reduced my level of gratitude.

If I was a hardened soldier, a spy, or one of those whisky-swilling detectives, I would have contained the groan. I would have tricked my captors about my state of consciousness and found a way to turn the tables. But I wasn't.

"Do not attempt to use your magic," a voice warned. A familiar British voice accompanied by the smell of formaldehyde. "The bracers we have layered on your hands will bring pain from the Mana you form."

"Don't think I could even if I wanted to," I said, prying my eyes open. I groaned as pricks of light slammed into my head, forcing my eyes closed again. I stayed lying on the floor, letting the cold of the concrete seep into my aching head. "I think I'll just stay here."

"Unfortunately, that will not be possible. Now that you are awake, you will need to speak to the Council." So saying, Bronislav picked me up.

The smell of rot and preserving liquids intensified while he hauled me to my feet. I could barely find my feet before he pushed me, mostly pulling me forward rather than letting me walk. The motion made my stomach lurch, and only discipline kept me from throwing up.

"Good. Do not throw up. I do not care to launder my clothing again," Bronislav said. "The Council still has not increased my laundry budget. Even if they have increased their… activities."

"I… thought you guys were good guys," I whispered, not liking the implications of his words. As he dragged me along, the new skin along my shoulder ripped open and a slow trickle of blood wet my jacket.

"We try. But the Nun'Yunu'Wi's dietary requirements are much stricter," Bronislav said. "We do what we can with my connections. But so many people want open casket funerals that acquiring bodies—especially those that fit requirements—can be difficult. And the butchering…"

"I don't really want to know," I whispered. "Just. Can you guys not eat me?"

He was silent.

"Fuck," I said.

In short order, I was brought to an all-too-familiar location. This time around, I was not left to stand but dumped onto a chair—an old school medieval-looking torture chair with restraining straps for arms and head. In short order, I was trussed up, though as I ran my fingers along the edge of the vinyl armrest, I realized something.

"This is a bondage chair!" I said. I mean, sure, it was great for restraining but I swear, if they hadn't cleaned it off properly, I was going to complain.

My shock and sudden exclamation threw my careful control of my stomach into turmoil and I found myself lurching forward, only to be brought up against the strap holding my head still as I tried to vomit. Dry heaving, some of the refuse bubbled up my mouth and spilled down my lips before rushing back down, throwing me into another paroxysm of coughing and spitting.

"Free him. Let him vomit. Then clean him," the Chair barked.

Bronislav was quick to follow his orders, releasing me to throw up then cleaning me up. The Nun'Yunu'Wi hissed and snapped his cane toward me, making my shirt burn off, along with the rest of the vomit. It cleansed me, though it scorched my skin too and left me screaming and thrashing, sending me into another paroxysm. Rather than wait for me to finish, another wave of magic flowed into me. This time around, I felt my head healing, my thoughts clearing. Surprisingly, the wound in my back and the blood that had escaped was not healed.

"I told you you should heal him. Mages are fragile," the troll growled.

"We should have just killed him," the Chair snapped. "We agreed to that. If the others learn—"

"They will not. Not even the Council can pierce my defenses," the Nun'Yunu'Wi said, laughing a little derisively at the vampire. "You worry too much."

"And you risk too much."

"For the jinn, this risk is nothing," the Nun'Yunu'Wi said.

"Enough. Let us get this over with," the troll said. "Many saw our fight. Some might suspect."

"Very well. Wizard." When the Nun'Yunu'Wi saw that it had my attention, it pointed at my finger. "Use your wish and release yourself from your previous wish."

"Or what?" I snorted at the trio. They couldn't hurt me. Not directly. Even now, Lily protected me. Protected me from—

A crowbar came down on my arm with full force, cracking the bones. I screamed, thrashing about but unable to move much. Bronislav looked back at his masters after the strike, stopped only by a raised hand.

"Your wish protects you from us. But we have many of the appropriate 'Level.'"

"Fuck."

"Yes." The Nun'Yunu'Wi leaned forward. "Save yourself some pain. I can heal you if you grow too damaged and you will repeat the pain. Again and again, till we get what we want. Why bother?"

"What—what do you want with Lily?" I said, doing my best to ignore the pain in my arm and the blood that ran down my back in fresh waves. Ignore the way I could tell even my normal Mana regeneration was being disrupted by the enchanted bracers. Ignore the welling feeling of helplessness.

"It is not your concern."

A nod and another strike. Except this time around, Bronislav hit me twice, cracking an upper arm and a rib before he was called off.

Once I was coherent again, when the waves of pain had subsided, I looked at the Nun'Yunu'Wi. "What does the Council want? You do know the ring goes to one person only?"

My words made Roland shift, but the Nun'Yunu'Wi laughed. "Did you think to sow discord among us?"

A gesture and pain came. This time, four strikes. Not all of them broke bones, but the pain was so great, it took me long minutes before I could focus again.

"Half-measures. Let me cut him up. Once I eat his foot in front of him, they always break," the troll was arguing with the Nun'Yunu'Wi.

"You know why cutting him will not work, Vallen," the Nun'Yunu'Wi snapped.

"Oh, yes. You and your fear of blood." Roland laughed, shaking its head. "How pitiful, to fear something so great."

"As if fearing sunlight was any better—"

"My lords," Bronislav spoke up, bringing the attention of the group back to me.

"Don't worry about me. I'll… wait," I said, trying for a smile and failing. The pain continued to radiate, the pulses of agony taking away my ability to plan. If not for the last while of training, I probably would not have been able to even speak that much.

"Make the wish."

I paused, considering. Make the wish. A wish. I could make a wish. Easy. Wish them gone. Wish them dead. Wish myself free even. Wish myself free…

"Okay," I said, looking up. "I wish—"

Before I could finish, the Nun'Yunu'Wi gestured and Roland cracked me across the face, shattering my jaw. I screamed, the strike throwing me back against the chair and nearly tipping it over. Pain, so much pain. And then, blessed darkness once again.

***

The next few hours were memorable, but not for the right reasons. The beating continued, interspersed with healing spells. It took about three tries before I realized that the son of a bitch was reading my mind—or a close facsimile of that—so that every time I tried to use the wish for anything other than what they wanted, I got smacked around. And while Lily might guess at my desires, until I voiced it out loud, she couldn't make it true.

I was no semi-mute hero, no tough-as-nails private eye or trained soldier. When I got tortured, I felt the pain and scream just like anyone else. If not for the last few weeks of training, I wouldn't have lasted even ten minutes. If not for Lily's notification, I'd have broken in twenty.

Active Quest: Last Till Help Arrives
Help is on the way. But it's taking time to get organized. You will need to hold out from the torture and refuse to make the wish until help arrives.
Requirement: -0:01:38
Reward: Rescue Attempt
Failure: Your Death. Loss of the Ring. Potential Armageddon.

It was those words I woke up to each time I was struck. That clock dominated my view and focused me whenever they struck me, when I felt the shattering of another bone. It was what I clung to when the pain of healing swept over me and my jaw and shattered pieces of my body stitched themselves back together.

There was only so much that magical healing could do. Only so much battering a body could take before even magic lost its effectiveness. Each time they broke something, each time my body bruised and blood vessels broke, pieces were left untreated, unfinished. Shards of bone lay amidst healed flesh, hurting and grating with each movement, each pulse of blood. My nose, shattered so many times that I made boxers look handsome, wheezed with each breath. My jaw, cracked again and again, was distorted. And my mind...

Multiple concussions in short order meant I was thinking feebly, barely able to focus on a single thought. It was perhaps because of that that the

Nun'Yunu'Wi could not read my mind any longer. When I could not focus on my own thoughts, how could another?

"Make the wish!" the Nun'Yunu'Wi insisted.

"Urgh… I…" I leaned over, my head freed from its strap after the fourth? fifth? beating to spit and throw up. I coughed and coughed again, throat both dry and wet with congealed blood.

My hesitation made Bronislav glare at me.

"Enough," Roland said. "He is barely coherent. You need to let him recover."

"I have healed him," the Nun'Yunu'Wi snapped.

"Repeatedly. The human body cannot take such abuse," Roland said.

"Oh, it can take more. Much more—"

"Screaming insanity is not the result we need. He must be coherent to say what we want him to say," Roland said. "Give him a few minutes. If he is unwilling to continue, you can continue the beating."

The Nun'Yunu'Wi stroked his hand in thought before he nodded. "Yes. A respite will make the agony afterward more pronounced."

"How much longer?" the troll, wandering back with a haunch of meat, asked, glancing at my broken form as he flopped onto his oversized seat.

While they waited for me to recover and I played broken—not that that was a particularly difficult act—Bronislav picked up a new cloth and wiped me down. He had been doing that repeatedly, keeping me clear of blood from the occasional bone that popped out, the accidentally bit tongue or split lip. For all the brutality Bronislav had inflicted upon me, his touch was soft, gentle as he cleaned me. It was… nice. Comforting. I found myself leaning into his hands, seeking warmth. Comfort. It had been hours, hours of abuse and pain and now…

"He is tougher than I expected," the troll said, glancing at me. "But I still think you should cut off a limb or two. Maybe the one in between—"

"We agreed that this is mine," the Nun'Yunu'Wi said.

"I thought it would take an hour at most. Sooner or later…"

In the corner of my eye, I saw the clock counting down. Changing.

0:0:44

0:0:43

A flicker and the timer changed again.

0:0:11

"What? They can look all they want. But our people have shown that they do not know where we are. Or what we do," the Nun'Yunu'Wi said. "There is no way for them to find us. My wards are—"

The Nun'Yunu'Wi never finished his words as he lurched backward as if he had been struck. Which, in a sense, he had been. His wards, the enchantments that protected this room from scrying and other forms of assault, crumpled like a

252

beer can in a frat boy's hand. A moment later, a portal opened, one that brought the light of day to the room, flooding it. Even before the portal had finished opening, a spear flew through the gap and slammed into the troll, pinning it to the wall. White fire—the flames of faith-based magic—burned around the wound and along the haft of the spear.

Roland screeched and threw himself away from the sunlight, bringing a jacket-filled hand up to his face as the vampire fled to the farthest corner of the room. Bronislav's eyes widened, hesitating over who to protect, and was rewarded for his hesitation by a blast of force magic that carried him back.

Congratulations! Quest Completed.
Reward: Rescue Attempt!

First to emerge from the Portal was Alexa wielding a pair of wands I had gifted her. She kept them leveled at Bronislav, sending the Frankenstein spinning away as he burnt and was smacked around by the fire and force magic. The moment she reached me though, she dropped the spent wands to work on my bindings.

Behind Alexa was Caleb, staff leveled at the Nun'Yunu'Wi as spell after spell formed and fired. It was a blitz of light and energy, Mana forming along spell formulas at a speed that was impossible to track. Even as distracted as I was, I couldn't help but note that Caleb was going with low-level spells instead of something more powerful.

"God, I'm so sorry, Henry! We tried to get here, but finding everyone…" Alexa said to me as she struggled to free me from the chair.

Everyone, to my surprise, included a tiny Pixie. Ela walked from the Portal too, her focus not on the others but the vampire. Instead of directly fighting him, she hurried around the portal with a bunch of mirrors, redirecting sunlight to trap Roland in his corner.

"It's fine," I said, touching my clouded head. I wheezed as I tried to breathe properly, then I looked at my ring. "Lily…"

The jinn popped into space right next to me, offering me a half-smile. "Hi, Henry. You got to go."

New Quest: Escape!
Your friends have arrived. Now it's time to go.
Time Limit: 00:02:11
Rewards: Freedom. Live for another day.
Failure: More enemies.

Rather than answer her, with both hands free and Alexa working on my feet, I turned to where Bronislav was picking himself off the floor. He'd looked better for sure, the majority of his shirt and jacket burnt off, exposed skin blackened and the stitching around his body torn. One entire flap of skin along his chest had slipped off, exposing blackened internal organs and copper wiring. But for all that damage, Bronislav was moving, dragging a lame foot over to us, the hated crowbar in hand.

I focused on the bar, then on Bronislav's grinning, savage face. And then… and then, my mind blanked. I only came to when I felt Alexa shoving against my shoulder, screaming into my face.

"Enough, Henry! Enough!" Alexa's voice was hoarse.

I blinked, and the break in my concentration saw the channeled Mana from my fingers die off. A smell assaulted my nose—not the piss and vomit, the blood that I had spilled, but the burnt smell of fat and skin, of crisped flesh. As Alexa retracted herself from in front of me, I saw the cause.

A burnt husk, a charred corpse. Skin turned to ashes, fat bubbling and organs shriveled, bones and metal wiring glowing. Beside it, the puddled remnants of the crowbar.

"Did I do that?" I said wonderingly.

"We got to go!" Ela screamed, already perched next to the Portal.

Lily was beside me, echoing Ela's words, a big flashing quest marker. I flinched, instinct making me grab and pull Alexa down beside me as my brain caught up with the answer.

Quest Failed: Escape!
Penalty: More Enemies!!!

The door leading to the room blew in. Reinforced wards, already weakened by our entry, were blasted apart. Ela, caught by the blast, was thrown through the opening she had been standing beside. The Portal flickered and slammed shut, the ritual holding it open disrupted on the other side. Caleb, caught by surprise, turned from his attack for a second—only to find the Nun'Yunu'Wi gone by the time he turned back.

As the wind and shattered remnants of the spell blew through all of us but for the jinn, it also destroyed and overturned the numerous mirrors El had laid out. Not that it mattered now that the portal was closed. Hugging Alexa, I rolled with the explosion, feeling barely healed old wounds and new ones bleeding.

Still, I was able to turn aside enough to see the doorway. To note the black hounds charging through only to be torn apart by the freed vampire. The pair of sidhe that strolled in, a pair of assault rifles to their shoulders, searched the room with precise motions, one of them targeting the troll that had finally freed himself and the other bringing its gun to bear on me. It fired immediately, only to have its bullets stopped.

Sidhe Lord (Level 184)
Out of Level attack blocked.

He snarled, stepping aside as he switched targets. "Knights. It's your turn!"

"We're coming, pagan monstrosity."

A quartet of mortal knights came rushing through the door. They had no guns, instead wielding melee weapons, the various sheaths where they carried additional magazines already empty. There was a story there, but one I had no time to learn. Not when Alexa shoved me off and stood, snatching her short spear from the floor and facing the quartet.

"Henry!" Lily called to me, and even through the chaos, I heard the jinn. Through all this, she stood. Untouched. Untouchable. Bullets flew and curved around her. Magic broke against an invisible ward, leaving her and her clothing unstained. "There's more coming."

I closed my eyes, my brain still muddled. The never-ending fire of assault weapons in an enclosed room beat upon my ears, against my chest like the tiny fists of a puppy. The smell of death and decay pervaded the room, my skin and muscles on fire from the repeated attacks. And in their corner, Caleb and the Nun'Yunu'Wi dueled, their magic pressing against that sense too.

It was too much. Too much.

My friends were trying to rescue me. My family. People who had given up time and safety. And I'd failed them, failed to get out when we should have. We were trapped. And I had nothing…

"Kill him. Before he makes a wish."

A spear, thrown at close range, was barely deflected by Alexa. It cut along my arm, tearing open a wound that I did not notice. Alexa, seeing me overwhelmed, fell back and pulled a sphere. She let it drop, and a small dome formed around me. A protective spell, one of Caleb's. Too complicated, wasteful. But still more powerful than anything I could do.

But there was something strange there. Something… I cocked my head as I realized that somehow, I'd heard those words. In all the noise. I'd heard…

Even through the glow of the protective ward, I spotted the jinn. Lily offered me a half-smile.

A wish. Simple.

"I wish…"

What?

I didn't know.

If I knew, I'd have made the wish before. To ask them gone? For what? Another day, another painful few hours. My enemies wanted me dead and would take it out on me and my friends if I wished their deaths. Their destruction. I had no time to come up with anything perfect, anything smart. No time to game the system, to figure out the right wording, the right way to do this. No time…

A wish. A single wish to make everything right. To fix… everything.

It was impossible. It always had been. That was why I'd never made the wish. How could a single wish fix anything? A single action? It can't. Nothing can.

Because the ills of the world, of existence were greater than any single action, any person.

All you can do was hope. And trust. That those around you would do the best they could.

"That you had my wish to use as you see fit, Lily."

A single wish. And trust. That was all there was. That was all there ever was.

Chapter 19

The moment the wish was made, silence spread across the entire battlefield of the room. It was not some weird movie effect, one of those unlikely silences that enveloped a battlefield because the director wanted to showcase an important moment. Lily flexed and suddenly, no one could move. A fraction of a second later, combatants were pulled apart, bullets moving through mid-air fell to the floor with a tinkle of falling rain, and Mana that had been gathering stilled.

"Well. That's enough of that," Lily said, straightening. When the troll tried something, she flicked a hand and squashed it against the wall, where it leaked blood. "Hush. All of you. This is my moment. And I won't have it spoiled."

"Lily?" I said, standing as I looked at the jinn, who seemed so different now.

Lily turned to look at me, no longer looking like a cute but somewhat scared gamer girl but an imperious queen. She was even taller than me now. As I glanced down, I realized why. The jinn was levitating, adding a couple of inches to her height. A snap of her fingers and the hoodie disappeared, as well as the slacks, and a regal gold-and-green gown appeared along with glittering jewelry.

"Much better. You really were slow. But you managed to do it," Lily said, looking at me.

"How—how are you able to do this?" I said, looking at the still-frozen fighters. At Alexa, who was taking the intermission in fighting to bandage her thigh. "You shouldn't be able to do this. The rules—"

"Are made by me. I just bent them," Lily said. In answer, another notification appeared.

Hidden Quest Completed: Give the Jinn a Wish
Rewards: ???

"What? That's not how that works. You always indicated what the quest rewards are!" I protested.

"Not always. Sometimes rewards are hidden if you haven't completed the prerequisites," Lily snapped at me. For a second, I saw my friend in the imperious supernatural queen, then she was back as she turned toward one of the sidhe that was rubbing at an amulet. "Stop that. It will not work, but it is annoying."

The sidhe stopped, a resigned look in its eyes. "What do you intend to do, jinn?"

"Do? Hmmm… so much. So very much. But I should finish my wish. Then I'll deal with you." Lily turned to me and gestured.

The ring on my finger flew from my hand—taking a little bit of skin with it, such was the force of its movement. The ring hovered next to Lily, glowing before her. Another gesture and the glow expanded, resolving into runic script, the packed-together spell formulas becoming legible as she kept expanding the script. It took up the entire room, and we still had to squint to make out even a portion of the script itself. Considering a single rune could be considered a sentence, the complexity of the enchantment packed into the ring made my head hurt.

"Incredible," Caleb breathed, his eyes flicking as he took in what he could.

"Are you freeing yourself, lady of fire and smoke?" the Nun'Yunu'Wi said, bowing deep from its waist. "It was only what I wanted to do. To free such a magnificent lady."

"Do you know, it's been tried before?" Lily said. "Wishing me free? It was one of the first things my followers tried." There was silence as Lily flicked a finger and a section of the spell formula was highlighted. "But they were smart. That is one of many things that cannot be wished for. Doing so forces me to end their lives."

The Nun'Yunu'Wi froze at her words while the Knights relaxed a little, the hard tension in their bodies disappearing. Relaxed, because the threat that was the jinn was gone—supposedly. Or at least, her being freed. Though I wondered if they considered—or cared—that their lives might be entirely forfeit at this point.

"What are you going to do?" I said as I hobbled over to Alexa and bent, taking hold of the end of the bandage that she'd been struggling to get wrapped properly.

The ex-Initiate flashed me a smile while I took over, and she found a healing potion in her jacket liner to chug. I focused on the bandage, noting how the blood still leaked. I didn't want to look at Lily, at the person I thought had been my friend. And who now looked or talked nothing like her. Who, I dreaded, might have tricked me.

"Mmmm… I cannot wish myself free. I cannot wish the stone apart. And my powers are still contained by this ring," Lily said, tapping her lips. "It's… annoying. Simple solutions have been blocked off for a long time. But I've had thousands of years to think about it. To test theories. To have other ring bearers try out other options." Lily let the silence grow. "To learn."

For two such innocuous words, they sent a shiver down all our backs.

Lily turned, looking around. Her gaze was distant, as if she was seeing things that I couldn't. "Well. I guess I should sort this out first. Give you your reward."

There was something in her voice that made my eyes widen.

"Stop!" Caleb shouted, lurching forward a half-inch before the spells holding him froze him.

I did not understand what he was screaming about, could not. Until I felt pain all over, all at once. Pain that came not just from my body but from my soul. I screamed, and then my body came apart.

***

I came back to my senses, still screaming, in a clearing, a lookout above the city. I was in the same position, hands splayed as if they were wrapping another person's leg. My chest heaved as I ran out of air, and I drew another breath to scream again. Only to find that I wasn't hurting. Not at all.

"Wha…?" I looked around at the slow-setting sun. At the white, fluffy clouds and the peaceful blue of the sky. The green of the grass, all the greener now after hours of harsh white light in a grey, concrete basement. Smells—normal, human, natural smells. And to my Mana Sense, the deep, deep upwelling of power coming from beneath me as multiple ley lines crossed over one another.

"There. That should do it," Lily said beside me.

I blinked, looking at the jinn. "Lily?"

"Sorry. I'm stretching the rules, but I need to make this wish soon," Lily said. "I've healed you. Your friends are back where they are meant to be. If this fails… well. You should run."

I nodded, knowing she was right. We'd had plans for if we had survived. If the ring was… well. Where was the ring? And then I saw it—around her finger.

"Time to try again," Lily said, raising the hand with the ring on it. The jinn stared at the ring, her voice far away as she contemplated things I could not hope to envision. "The problem with enchantments, no matter how powerful, no matter how smart their creators were, is that they are static. And.

"I.

"Am.

"Not."

Light. A soundless thunder, one that shook my chest and newly healed ear drums. That stole my breath and sent my Mana Senses abuzz. I felt it, the war between her and the ring. Her strength, pitched directly at the ring, changing it. Altering it. Flexing the spell and the enchantment.

I could not tell what it was she did, though I knew she was trying to twist the enchantment itself. Perhaps she was trying to break it, because I felt the strain that what Lily was doing was bringing to reality itself. I felt the power that she drew from the ley lines to assault the ring with, and I felt how it made my senses hurt, how the Mana conduits in my body expanded and soaked up the energy.

Rather than risk being burnt out, knowing I could do little, I retreated. Back and back again, even as Lily lit a beacon to anyone in the world that something momentous, something world-changing was happening.

No surprise that others came. A stray breeze, and a man with an eyepatch on a horse was there. A rumble of earth, and a stone rose. A stone that had hints of someone, something trapped within. The earth rippled, and from a crack that smelled of brimstone, a horned, goat-footed creature walked. Clouds gathered and formed more faces, some with long whiskers and wrinkled brows, another pudgy, long-lobed, and laughing. More. So many more gathered.

Just a single presence was enough to overload my senses. I could not stare at any one of them, could not hear them. Their presence was like a thousand pounds on my chest, forcing me to gasp as I tried to breathe. Tried… and failed.

Then it was gone. A delicate hand was on my shoulder, pushing away the presences. I turned and saw a fair lady clad in white robes who floated on a lotus blossom to place a hand on my shoulder. The smile on her face was kind and gentle, a promise of safety and mercy.

"Thank—thank you," I said once I could breathe again.

"No thanks is required." But as polite as she was, as nice as she was, I could tell her attention was not on me.

So I turned back to the show.

Not a single personage, not a single player moved to interfere. Where Lily stood fighting her battle, none took part. She struggled against the binding that held her still alone. Pitting thousands of years of knowledge against the spell, pitting everything she had against it. Altering rune by rune. Forcing a change. And all the while, the ring glowed and power welled.

For hours she stood there, power welling, the center of attention. Hours where, to mortal eyes, nothing changed. And yet we stood in silent vigil. The sun set, the moon rose, and still she stood.

And then, as suddenly as it had started, the Mana swell disappeared — as did Lily. One moment, she was there, standing by herself, then she was gone. The sudden change made me lurch forward as if a rug had been pulled out from underneath me.

A simultaneous exhalation of relieved tension rose from those around. A few of the personages looked at one another. Some glared. Others grouped up, chatting. Most just disappeared, including the lady who had saved me. I was not surprised. She had much to do. And what she did, she did not do for gratitude.

I stood there. Ringless. Alone. As I reached out to that bundle of power where my character sheet and my party interface was, I found it gone. Empty.

Truly alone then.

Epilogue

"I said no, Caleb." I cradled the phone to my head, while I attempted to juggle the call, my keys, and takeout as I stood before the door to my apartment. My new apartment, one that I'd found after spending over a month looking for.

The door was yanked open, revealing Alexa. She limped back to couch. "Is that Caleb? Tell him no. And I hope you bought extra egg rolls!"

"See? Even Alexa says no. I'm not joining the Council, no matter what they say." I listened to Caleb as I kicked the door closed and walked to the kitchen to drop off the food. "I don't really have that much to show them anyway. Lily left me with the spells she'd given me, but that was it. I don't have any more lost arts to offer." I listened a little more, nodding to his words and rolling my eyes as I sat the takeout boxes down on the kitchen counter. "Yeah, I'll see you Saturday for game night. Byyyye!"

Heaving a sigh of relief, I made sure the call was killed then stuffed the phone back in my front pocket. In short order, I had a pair of heaping plates of food that I carried over to Alexa.

"Think they believe you?" Alexa asked.

"Of course not. But without the ring, I'm just a little more powerful Mage. Not worth actually fighting for." I shrugged and handed Alexa her plate. "So long as I avoid the guys who are still holding a little grudge over who I killed, I should be good. Thankfully, they were all low-Level guys like me."

We ate for a bit, contemplating the fallout right after the fight. There'd been quite a few glares and shouted recriminations, but considering the fact that an all powerful jinn was loose, people had better things to do than throw accusations around. There were defences to raise, people to warn. In the chaos, we'd managed to sneak away.

"Do you miss it?" Alexa asked, raising an eyebrow.

"What? My powers?" I shook my head. "It was fun, playing the game. Making my life a game. But the consequences…" I recalled my family, the shell-shocked look on their faces when I met them. The screaming and tantrums. My father refusing to speak with me because of the way I'd put them all in danger. And my friends – injured, outcast, lost. "I think I like my games virtual."

Alexa gave me a half-smile, a trace of sadness settling around us as we remembered our friend.

"How's the leg?" I asked to change the topic. A few days ago, we'd been running another assignment, taking on a risky hunt for an escaped min-hydra pet. Not only had we been required to find it, we had to return it unharmed. Which meant Alexa had to get close – resulting in the bite. Unfortunately, hydra venom wasn't something you wanted a healing potion on.

"Better. The venom is mostly gone," Alexa said. "Another day and we could probably use a healing potion to fix this."

"Good, good." I nodded.

"You just want me to get back to earning my share."

"Well, we do have a few debts…"

Patching our lives together after the incident meant that we'd had to explain a "gas explosion" in our apartment as well as replace all our belongings. Not surprisingly, our renter's insurance hadn't paid out—what with us disappearing for months after the explosion. If not for some minor tweaking by a few friends, we would be in even worse trouble with the authorities.

As it was, we were just scorned and in debt.

"You okay, Henry?" Alexa said, eyes narrowing.

"I'm fine. Why?"

"You bought enough for three." Alexa pointed at the kitchen.

I turned, staring at the takeout. "No, that's for… after."

"Uh huh," Alexa said.

Thankfully she decided not to pursue the matter. Not as if we hadn't had this talk before. In strained silence, we focused on dinner. It was part habit – buying enough for three – and part… hope? Wish? It was a fool's hope.

***

Starlight twinkled as it entered our window, playing across the coffee table. In her bedroom,

---

Alexa slept, thanks to the drugs for the pain from the wound that refused to heal fully. I sat in the living room, a hand caressing the gaming laptop. The one I'd bought a week ago and I'd never even cracked open.

"Stupid. It's just a game…" I swore at myself, fed up, and finally cracked it open. I tapped the power button and sat back, watching the computer boot up. Watched it get ready.

A feeling of dread, of fear washed over me. And even as it asked me to input a password, I reached forward to slam it shut.

"Hey! I was playing that."

"No, you're not. I don't even have any games downloaded," I retorted automatically. And then froze.

Slowly, I turned sideways to see a familiar figure seated beside me. A figure in a hoodie and jeans, brown hair escaping around the raised hood. A mocking half-smile on her face and a familiar ring on her hand.

"Hey, Henry. Long time no see."

The End

Author's Note

Ending this series was a bittersweet experience. I kind of knew this as going to happen, ever since I wrote the first book. Many of the events changed on me, the timing and the format, but the ending – with Lily being freed was always going to happen.

This is my first series that I've ever written 'The End' for. First series to put to bed, to set aside. Are there stories still in this universe? Yes. But, this is a good place to let Henry, Lily and Alexa stay. At least for a while.

I learnt a lot writing this series. A Gamer's Wish first released in March 2018. It's been nearly two years since then, and it's been a learning experience as I have written and developed more. Henry's story came from a single question – what happens when a gamer gets a magic ring and wishes for magic? Some characters, well, they made themselves known with a spearpoint and just refused to leave. Others faded away off, their part played. But the series and the characters will live on.

Really, I'm not sure what else to say but I hope you enjoyed the series. It was fun writing and one day, if enough people ask for it, I might write a sequel.

In the meantime, I have other series including my A Thousand Li (my cultivation xianxia series), the Adventures on Brad (a more traditional LitRPG fantasy) and the System Apocalypse (a post-apocalyptic scifi-fantasy LitRPG). Book one of each series follow:

- A Thousand Li (a cultivation series inspired by Chinese wuxia and xianxia novels)
https://readerlinks.com/l/729231
- A Healer's Gift (Book 1 of the Adventures on Brad)
https://books2read.com/healers-gift
- Life in the North (An Apocalyptic LitRPG)
https://readerlinks.com/l/729295

For more great information about LitRPG series, check out the Facebook groups:
- Gamelit Society
https://www.facebook.com/groups/LitRPGsociety/
- LitRPG Books
https://www.facebook.com/groups/LitRPG.books/

If you'd like to support me directly, I now have a Patreon page where previews of all my new books can be found!
- https://www.patreon.com/taowong

About the Author

Tao Wong is an avid fantasy and sci-fi reader who spends his time working and writing in the north of Canada. He's spent way too many years doing martial arts of many forms, and having broken himself too often, he now spends his time writing about fantasy worlds.

For updates on the series and his other books (and special one-shot stories), please visit the author's website: http://www.mylifemytao.com

Subscribers to Tao's mailing list will receive exclusive access to short stories in the Thousand Li and System Apocalypse universes: https://www.subscribepage.com/taowong

Or visit Tao's Facebook Page: https://www.facebook.com/taowongauthor/

About the Publisher

Starlit Publishing is wholly owned and operated by Tao Wong. It is a science fiction and fantasy publisher focused on the LitRPG & cultivation genres. Their focus is on promoting new, upcoming authors in the genre whose writing challenges the existing stereotypes while giving a rip-roaring good read.

For more information on Starlit Publishing, visit their website:
https://www.starlitpublishing.com/

You can also join Starlit Publishing's mailing list to learn of new, exciting authors and book releases.
https://starlitpublishing.com/newsletter-signup/

A Thousand Li: The First Step Sample Chapter

"Cultivation, at its core, is a rebellion."

Waiting for their reaction, the thin, mustached older teacher stared at the students seated cross-legged before him. Apparently not seeing the reaction he wanted, the teacher flung the long, trailing sleeves of the robes he wore with a harrumph and continued his lecture. Keeping his expression entirely neutral, Long Wu Ying could not help but smirk within. Such a statement, no matter how contentious, lost its impact after daily repetition over the course of a decade.

"Cultivation demands one to defy the very heavens itself. Each step on the path of cultivation sets you on the road to rebellion to defy the heavens, to defy our king. It is only by his good graces and his belief in the betterment of the kingdom that you are allowed to cultivate."

Wu Ying struggled to keep his face neutral as the refrain continued. Usually, he could tune out the teacher until it came time to cultivate, but today he struggled to do so. Today, he could not help but rebut the teacher in his mind. Teaching the villagers how to cultivate was a purely practical decision on the king's part. Most children would achieve at least the first level of Body Cleansing by their twelfth birthday. That allowed them to grow stronger and healthier, even on the little food they had left after the state, the nobles, and the sects had taken their portion.

"The beneficent auspices of the king allow you to cultivate, study the martial arts, and defend yourself. It is only because of his belief that each village must be a strong member of the kingdom that we have grown to the heights we have!"

It had nothing to do with the desire to begin training the villagers to be useful soldiers in the never-ending wars. Or to ensure that the village was not robbed of the grain they farmed by the bandits that seemed to grow in number every year. Or the fact that less than two hundred li[1] away, the Verdant Green Waters Sect watched over them all, searching for new recruits.

"Now, begin!"

Exhaling a grateful breath that Master Su had finally finished, Wu Ying tried to focus his mind on cultivating. That he respected his teacher was without question, but Master Su was a stickler for the rules, which required him to give the same lecture every single time. Even a saint would find it hard to listen after a while. And Wu Ying was many things, but a Saint he most definitely was not.

It didn't help that the state was obviously of two minds about cultivation itself. The three pillars of a kingdom were the government, the populace, and the cultivating sects. A weakness in any of the three would make a kingdom vulnerable. For a kingdom to be stable, each pillar needed to be as strong, as upright and firm, as the others. If any

---

[1] Half a kilometer or roughly a third of a mile

278

single pillar grew too high, it would eventually lead to the collapse of the kingdom.

Because of that, a wise ruler would support the development of their populace through cultivation, the surest and best form of developing an individual. But a single cultivator, if they achieved true power, could—and had, historically—overturn governments. And so, the state would always view cultivators and cultivation with some degree of distrust.

"Wu Ying. Focus!" Master Su said.

Wu Ying grimaced slightly before he made his face placid again. Master Su was right. He could think about all these thoughts another time. This was the time for cultivation. The time a villager had to cultivate was limited and precious. Stray thoughts were wasteful.

Drawing a deep breath, Wu Ying exhaled through his nose. The first step in cultivation was to clear the mind. The second was to control his breathing, for breath was the source of all things. At least in the Yellow Emperor's Cultivation Method that had been passed down and used by all peasants in the kingdom of Shen.

The first step on the road to cultivation was that of bodily purification. To ascend, to gain greater strength and develop one's chi, a cultivator needed to purify their body of the wastes that accumulated. Starting the process young helped to reduce the amount of such waste build up and speeded up the progress of cultivation. That was

---

why every villager began cultivating as soon as possible. Those children who achieved the first level of Body Cleansing at a young age were hailed as prodigies.

Wu Ying was not considered a prodigy. Wu Ying had started cultivating at the age of six, like every other child in the village, and through hard work and discipline, he'd managed to achieve not just the first level of Body Cleansing but the second. True prodigies, at Wu Ying's age of seventeen, would already be at the fourth or fifth stage. Each of the twelve stages of Body Cleansing saw the conscious introduction and cleansing of another major chi meridian. When an individual had consciously introduced and could control the flow of chi through all twelve major pathways, all the stages of Body Cleansing were considered complete.

Wu Ying breathed in then out, slowly and rhythmically. He focused on the breath, the flow of air into his lungs, the way it entered his body as his stomach expanded and his chest filled out. Then he exhaled, feeling his stomach contract, the diaphragm moving upward as air circulated away.

In time, Wu Ying moved his focus away from breathing toward his dantian. Located below his belly button, in the space just slightly below his hip line and a few inches beneath the surface of his body, the lower dantian was the core of the Yellow Emperor's Cultivation Method. From there, through the flow and consolidation of one's internal chi, one would progress.

Once again, Wu Ying felt the mass of energy that was his dantian. As always, it was large in size but low in density, uncompacted and diffuse. His job was to gently nudge the flow of energy through his body's meridians, to send it on a major circulation through his body. In the process, his body sweated, as the normally docile chi moved through his body, cleansing and scouring away the impurities of life. In time, Wu Ying's normal sweat mixed with the impurities in his body, flowing from his pores. The rancid, bitter odor from Wu Ying's body mixed with the similar pungence coming from the rest of the class, a stench that even the open windows of the building could do little to disperse.

***

Deep in the process of cultivating, none of the students noticed the rancid smell, leaving only Master Su to suffer as he watched over the teenagers. Master Su had long gotten used to the offensive odor that he would be forced to endure for the next few hours as each of the classes progressed. It was a fair trade though, for Master Su received ten tael[2] of silver and, most

---

[2] A measurement of weight. Roughly 37.5 grams

importantly, a Marrow Cleansing pill each month for his work.

Deep in their cultivation, none of the students moved when a young man shook and convulsed. But Master Su took action, flashing over to the boy with a tap of his foot. Paired fingers raised as Master Su studied the thrashing boy before they darted forward, striking in rapid succession a series of acupressure points along the body. After the third strike, the convulsing slowed then stopped before the boy tipped over, coughing out blood.

"Foolish. Pushing to open the second meridian channel when you have not finished cleansing the first!" Master Su berated the boy, shaking his head. "Get up. Begin cultivating properly. You will stay here an extra hour."

"But…" the boy protested weakly but quieted at Master Su's glare.

"Foolish child!" Master Su growled as he stomped back to his station in front of the class. If he had not been there, the boy would likely have damaged himself permanently. Master Su watched as the boy wiped his mouth clear of blood before he snorted. Luckily, Master Su had been able to quell the rampaging chi flow, but the boy would likely have to spend the next few weeks on light duty at his farm. A bad time for that, considering the planting season they were in. "Stupid."

As the hour set aside for the teenagers to cultivate came to an end and the morning sun cast long shadows on the small village, the village bell rang. Master Su frowned slightly then smoothed his face as the students broke free from their cultivation trances one by one. It would never do for the students to see his concern.

"The session is over. Line up when you are done," Master Su commanded before he walked out of the small, single-room building that made up his school.

Outside, the teacher walked forward slightly, turning his head from side to side before he spotted the growing dust cloud.

"Master Su." Tan Cheng, the tall village head, came up to Master Su.

As the two individuals in the sixth level of the Body Cleansing stage, the pair shared the burden of guarding the village from external threats. It helped that Chief Tan was a lover of tea like Master Su.

"Chief Tan," Master Su greeted. "What is it?"

"The army recruiters," Chief Tan said, his eyes grave.

Master Su could not help but wince. This was the third time in as many years that the army had recruited from their village. The conscripts from the first year had yet to return, though news of deaths had trickled back. The war between their state of Shen and the state of Wei had dragged on, bringing misery to everyone.

"They're going to raise the taxes again then," Master Su said, trying to keep his tone light. Each year that the war dragged on, the taxes grew higher. He wondered how many the army would take this time and did not envy his friend. The first time the army arrived, they had filled the requirements with volunteers. The second time they came, each household that had more than one son and had yet to send a volunteer had sent their sons. This time, there would be no easy choices.

"Most likely." Chief Tan chewed on his lip slightly. As the rest of the villagers slowly streamed in from the surrounding fields, he looked around then looked down, avoiding the expectant gazes of the parents. Whatever came next, few would be happy.

***

"What is it?" Qiu Ru asked. The raven-haired beauty of the class prodded Wu Ying in the back as she tried to peer past the crowd of students who had gathered around the windows. Giving up, she prodded Wu Ying once more in the back to get him to answer.

"The army," Wu Ying finally answered.

As her eyes widened, he admired the way it made them shine—before he squashed his burgeoning feelings again. Qiu Ru had made it quite clear last summer festival that she had no interest in him. Now, Wu Ying had his sights set on Gao Yan. Even if Gao Yan was shorter, plumper, and had a bad tendency to forget to brush her teeth. That was life in the village—your choices were somewhat limited.

"Are they bringing back the volunteers?" Qiu Ru said.

"No. They're too early for that," Cheng Fa Hui said.

Wu Ying glanced at his friend, who had hung back with the rest of them. Not that Fa Hui needed to be up front to see what was happening. He towered over the entire group by a head. All except Wu Ying, who only lost to him by a handbreadth.

"If the army was returning our people, it would be before the winter," Fa Hui said. "That way the lord would not need to feed them."

Wu Ying grimaced and shot a look around the room, relaxing slightly when he saw that Yin Xue had not come to class today. As the nearest village to Lord Wen's summer abode, all the villagers dealt with Lord Wen and his son regularly. Truth be told, Yin Xue did not need to come to their village class, but the boy seemed to take pleasure in showcasing his ability over the peasants. As the son of the local lord, Yin Xue had access to a private cultivation tutor, spiritual herbs, and good food—all of which had allowed him to progress to Body Cleansing four already. In common parlance, he was what was known as a false dragon—a "forced" genius, rather than one who had achieved the heights of his cultivation by genius alone.

If Yin Xue had heard Fa Hui... Wu Ying mentally shuddered at the thought. Still, it was not as if Fa Hui was wrong. If the war was over, it made sense to make the villagers feed the returned sons rather than pay for hungry mouths over the winter.

"Are they here for us then?" Wu Ying mused. That would make sense.

After saying the words out loud, he noticed how the rest of the class stiffened. Before he could say anything to comfort them, Master Su called them out of the building.

Once the students had lined up outside, Wu Ying could easily see the army personnel, two of which were speaking with Chief Tan, while the others watched over the conscripts. As it was still early in the morning, the army had only managed to visit one other village thus far, and as such, there were only twenty such conscripts standing together. Yin Xue sat astride a horse, beside the conscripts but not part of them.

Wu Ying had to admit, the members of the army looked dashing in their padded undercoats, dark lamellar armor, and open-faced helms. But having watched two other groups leave and not return, with only rumors of the losses trickling back via the same recruiters and the itinerant merchant, much of the prestige and glory of joining the army had faded.

"Men, Lord Wen has sent his men to us once again. We are required to send twenty strong conscripts to join the king's army this year." Before the crowd could grasp the significance of the number, Chief Tan announced, "All sons from families who have not sent a child to the front, step forward."

Wu Ying stepped forward. As the only surviving son of his family, he had been safe from the recruiters beforehand. Along with Wu Ying, another six men stepped forward.

"All sons from families with more than one son in the village, step forward," Chief Tan announced.

This time, there was some confusion, but it was soon sorted out with some students pushed forward and others drawn back. By now, Wu Ying counted seventeen "volunteers."

"Why not daughters?" Qiu Ru called.

Wu Ying could not help but grimace at her impertinent words. As the local beauty, Qiu Ru had managed to get away with more impertinent comments than others. Interrupting the Chief while he was speaking was a new high.

"The army is looking for men!" Chief Tan snapped. "Qiu Jan! See to your daughter!"

"This is foolish!" Qiu Ru said.

When Chief Tan began to speak, he was silenced by a raised hand of the lieutenant, whose gaze raked over Qiu Ru. "You are quite the beauty. But our men do not need wives."

The hiss from the crowd was loud even as Qiu Ru flushed bright red at the insult.

"We are here to find soldiers. And you are, what? Body Cleansing one? Women are no use to us as soldiers until at least Body Cleansing four!"

Still flushed, Qiu Ru moved to speak, but her mother had managed to make her way over to the impertinent girl and gripped her arm. With a yank of her hand, the mother pulled Qiu Ru back. For a time, the lieutenant looked over the group, seeing that no one else was liable to interrupt, before he looked at Chief Tan.

"Tan Fu, Qiu Lee, Long Mao. Join the others," Chief Tan said softly.

Everyone knew why he had chosen the three, of course. Their families had been gifted with more than three surviving sons. Even now, their parents would have a single son left to work the farm, turn the earth. A good thing. Better than the families that were left without any. If you didn't consider the fact that now, three of their sons were fighting a war that none of them ever wanted.

"Good," the lieutenant said as his gaze slid over the new conscripts.

Wu Ying looked to the side as well, offering Fa Hui a tight smile as he saw his big friend look sallow and scared.

"Conscripts, return to your homes and collect your belongings. You will not be back for many months. Bring what you need. We will march in fifteen minutes. Gather at first bell," the lieutenant said.

The students stared at one another, looking at the few members of the class that were left, then at the other children. Wu Ying sighed and clapped Fa Hui on the shoulder, giving the giant a slight shove to send him toward his family. As if the motion was a signal, the group broke apart, the teenager's faces fixed as they moved to say their final goodbyes.

###

Read more about Wu Ying in book 1 of my Cultivation Series!

A Thousand Li: The First Step
https://readerlinks.com/l/971660

www.ingramcontent.com/pod-product-compliance
Lightning Source LLC
Chambersburg PA
CBHW060908210726
48293CB00006B/2017